New
cc WES ⊘ **WESTERN**

JW

Bmc

JM

D W

NEWARK PUBLIC LIBRARY-NEWARK, OHIO 43055

P9-CRC-825

WITHDRAWN

Large Print Pai
Paine, Lauran.
Thunder Valley /

B H

NEWARK PUBLIC LIBRARY
NEWARK, OHIO

GAYLORD M

THUNDER VALLEY

Also by Lauran Paine
in Thorndike Large Print ®

The Open Range Men
The Taurus Gun
Nightrider's Moon
The Blue Basin Country
Spirit Meadow
The New Mexico Heritage
Peralta Country
Custer Meadow
Arizona Panhandle

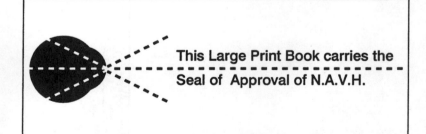

This Large Print Book carries the
Seal of Approval of N.A.V.H.

THUNDER VALLEY

Lauran Paine

Thorndike Press • Thorndike, Maine

Copyright © 1993 by Lauran Paine.

All rights reserved.

All the characters and events portrayed in this work are fictitious.

Thorndike Large Print ® Western Series edition published in 1993 by arrangement with Walker Publishing Company, Inc.

The tree indicium is a trademark of Thorndike Press.

Set in 16 pt. News Plantin by Warren Doersam.

This book is printed on acid-free, high opacity paper. ∞

Library of Congress Cataloging in Publication Data

Paine, Lauran.
    Thunder Valley / Lauran Paine.
      p. cm.
    ISBN 1-56054-720-0 (alk. paper : lg. print)
    1. Large type books.   I. Title.
    [PS3566.A34T48 1993b]
    813'.54—dc20

                                                 93-1385
                                                CIP

THUNDER VALLEY

NEWARK PUBLIC LIBRARY
NEWARK, OHIO 43055-5054

Large Print Pai
Paine, Lauran.
Thunder Valley /

5930871

CHAPTER 1

Anna Marie

Two years after the Custer debacle in Montana, while an outraged nation was pressing for the kind of concerted retaliation that eventually resulted in defeat and near annihilation of tribesmen everywhere west of the Missouri River, Frederick Miller — born Muller — died in the large bedroom of his ranch headquarters in the Conejo country. This area of New Mexico Territory was particularly subject to Indian depredations, having been the hunting and raiding grounds for generations of Apaches, Kiowas, Comanches — as well as far-ranging Cheyennes, Sioux, Crows, and an assortment of other tribesmen. Most of New Mexico was an ideal raiding country; it was largely open country with excellent visibility for miles, which made it possible for hard-riding and hard-hitting warriors to raid almost with impunity because they usually could see posse riders and soldiers before they themselves were seen.

But by 1878, most redskin scourges had been decimated, corralled, and shipped to reservations, or had scattered in small groups either into the mountains or down over the line into Old Mexico, where they could, and did, continue raiding, plundering, and murdering for many years, in part because of Mexican laws that prohibited ownership of firearms under penalty of death, edicts that left self-protection seriously ineffective.

But in the Conejo country of New Mexico, the raiding and killing had begun to diminish. What raids occasionally occurred in the Conejo country were mostly at night when a few head of cattle were driven off to feed starving tribesmen. The stockmen could stand the loss, most of them had thousands of acres of grassland and hundreds of head of cattle, but the point was simply that those annoying raids by destitute tribesmen were a lingering condition of warfare between the races. In retaliation, cowmen had banded together to seek out and destroy Indian villages, camps, and to attack without mercy bands they came across who were on the move.

The year Frederick Miller died peaceably in bed, with scars from many battles, not always against Indians, the Conejo was reasonably tamed. At least there had been no Indian skirmishes for some time, but the hair-triggered populace carried the war-years' temperament long after the last warrior had been killed. Gunmanship remained a way of life, and sometimes the lawful and the lawless seemed barely distinguishable, as the Far Westerners continued their frontier existence, little affected even by the laws and edicts from the nation's capital.

Frederick Miller had lived during the harsh, dangerous period of pioneering. He had been a bull of a man with stubborn zeal, otherwise he would never have been able to beat back the challenges that faced him and built up a ranch with many sections of good grassland, hundreds of head of cattle, a remuda of selectively up-bred saddle and harness stock. The home place, the headquarters of his vast ranch, was on a slight eminence with shaggy old cottonwood trees around the yard, outbuildings that included a shoeing shed, bunkhouse, cookshack, wagon and buggy shed, and a large barn made of massive logs brought from mountains some thirty-five miles away.

The main house was long, entirely surrounded by a roofed-over veranda, built mostly of adobe with walls three feet thick as protection from the fierce heat of New Mexican summers. The furnishing had been chosen by Fred Miller's wife, Anna Marie, a native Texan Fred had met and courted years ago when he was in Texas buying herds of cattle to be trailed to the Conejo. The only objection Anna Marie's kinsmen had had to the marriage was the difference in age; Fred was forty when they were married, Anna Marie had been twenty-five. But Fred had been a robust, hard-living individual in the prime of life, handsome, powerfully built, full of confidence, and on the way to becoming a wealthy rancher.

After his passing Anna Marie had mourned. She had also felt apprehensive about having the sole responsibility for a huge ranch. In the Conejo country, men shook their heads, while their womenfolk fiercely hoped she would prove capable.

She did. The three Mexican vaqueros who were permanent hired riders did the same chores for Anna Marie they had done for years for her husband, and since cattle ranching was largely a matter of repetition — marking and branding in springtime, culling in late fall, making up drives to railhead before winter, holding back the best heifers to replace old cows — she had become thoroughly familiar with the routine. For about a year everything went smoothly.

One afternoon her Mexican *mayordomo,* Hernando Iturbide, came to the main house to tell her someone was trapping horses on

10

the northeastern range, had built a mustang trap out there at a sump spring, and although Hernan' had wasted an hour waiting for someone to appear at the camp, he had not seen the trespasser.

Anna Marie shrugged and said that whoever he was, he probably did not know he was on private land.

Hernan' had nodded about that, but with reservations. The sixty-year-old vaquero was shrewd and experienced. Although the *mayordomo* did not mention it, wild-horse hunters scouted up many miles of countryside before setting up traps, and the trespasser's camp was no more than four miles from the ranch yard.

Anna Marie seemed to dismiss the trespasser. It was late spring, the cattle had been worked through more than a month earlier, so her concern was screw worms, sore-footed bulls, and rain. Mostly rain. If it did not arrive, the more southerly rangeland would dry up and wither early.

Hernan' returned to the bunkhouse to shrug off the questions of the other two riders. "She did not say we were to do nothing, but that was her attitude," he told them in Spanish.

For several days the essential work went forward. It consisted mainly in riding, watching the cattle for sickness or for hung-up calves among the heifers, shooting the occasional wolf or coyote hanging on the edge of a herd. It was routine, but Hernan', who was fully knowledgeable about mustangers and other encroachers, rode back to a low swell east of the trespasser's camp, and waited in the underbrush most of the afternoon until a horseman came loping from the north.

The gringo he saw was not particularly tall but powerfully muscled and not as young as Hernan' had expected, since catching wild horses was a young man's profession.

The man rode a leggy bay horse, probably at least half thoroughbred, and from its appearance able to outrun a wild horse even with a man on his back.

Hernan' got comfortable and watched the man examine his trap, look for tracks of horses entering it to get to water, and dump a bedroll beside a stone ring used for cooking. Wherever the bedroll had been used most recently, perhaps scouting the land for bands of mustangs, it was obviously now to become part of a permanent camp.

Hernan' rode back, met his companions, and on the ride back to the yard told them what he had seen, and what he had deduced from it, which was simply that the trespasser was not in any hurry to leave.

He told that to Anna Marie the same evening

12

and this time she seemed annoyed, but she still seemed to shrug off the transgression, so Hernan' reminded her as tactfully as he could, that her husband had never tolerated any kind of infringement on his ranch.

To this she had said, "Are there mustangs out there?"

Hernan' shook his head. "Not that I've seen. Not in several years."

"Then he will eventually give up and go away, won't he?"

Hernan' nodded stiffly. "*Señora,* our loose stock is out there."

"But they're branded, Hernan'."

The range boss did not yield. He stood gazing steadily at his attractive employer, expressionless and silent.

She faintly frowned. "A horse thief, Hernan'?"

The *mayordomo* shrugged.

Anna Marie frowned. "Can you watch him?"

Hernan' smiled broadly, showing strong white teeth.

Two days later he was back in the underbrush, but this time he got a shock when he saw the stranger ride up to his camp with two other people. A younger man on a worn-down old gray horse and an even younger girl riding a stocking-footed chestnut gelding who would

have been handsome if his ribs weren't showing through a dull, rough coat.

Hernan' watched as the mustanger helped
them with their bedrolls and saddlebags. He
watched the man show them his horse trap
and left the girl there at the spring while he
and the youth returned to the fire ring to make
coffee and hoecakes.

He sat up there in the brush so long the
sun was passing overhead before he realized
how long he'd been there. He went back, unhob-
bled his horse, and rode home without haste
puzzling over what he had seen.

When he told Anna Marie, this time her
reaction was positive. She said, "In the morning we will all ride over there."

Hernan' returned to the bunkhouse.
Gregorio Paredes, the vaquero who had one
eye that moved independently of the other
eye, smiled as he put platters of tough meat,
tortillas, and beans on three plates for his companions at the scarred old bunkhouse table.

Hernan' had something positive to report,
and filled the men in on the situation. Unlike
gringo range men, the vaqueros had had no
difficulty transferring their loyalty from the
dead *patrón* to his wife.

As Gregorio returned to the stove for the coffeepot he said, "Maybe they plan to start a set-
tlement out there. Maybe there will be others."

14

José Elizondo, a short, beefy, light-com-plexioned man, spoke around a mouthful of supper. "Not if the *patrón* was alive they wouldn't." José was said to be the son of a prominent *pronunciado* in Old Mexico who had been caught on a beach and shot to death for returning after being exiled.

The discussion for the balance of the evening went back to the condition of cattle, the dearth of scavenging wolves and coyotes, and finally, before they retired, to the need for rain.

The following morning they saddled their animals and the favorite of Anna Marie, an even-tempered gelding. The dark sorrel with a flaxen mane and tail had been a present from her husband three years earlier.

If Anna Marie noticed that her riders had booted carbines as well as the customary cartridge belt and Colt, she did not mention it as they left the yard in the cool of early morning.

She carried no gun. She owned several, including one with a pearl handle. The only time Anna Marie rode with a weapon was on those rare occasions when she had to ride the farthest northern, eastern, and westerly foothills and mountains. There were wolves and bear up there. Wolves faded before horsemen but a bear marked a definite territory and was liable to attack trespassers, two-legged or four-legged.

They left the yard at a dead walk and held to that gait for half an hour before boosting their mounts over into a rocking-chair lope, the preferred gait of horsemen. Half an hour into the ride Hernan' nodded to Anna Marie and loped ahead to guide the others up atop the brushy swell that had been his point of vantage.

Up there he showed them where to hobble their animals, then led them through the brush by following game trails until they could see the horse trap and the camp.

Anna Marie's surprise showed in her expression, not so much at the three strangers around the stone ring as at the permanent way the mustanger had built his trap around her spring.

She hunkered down with her riders and watched the girl fill the coffee cups of the men. She speculated that the girl's age must be under eighteen, although she was physically mature. And pretty. The younger man was perhaps a year or two older than the girl. The mustanger had gray at the temples. He had slightly hawkish features and was easy in his movements although he was muscular and sturdy.

José Elizondo brushed Hernan's arm and

pointed. After a moment Hernan' leaned over and whispered to Anna Marie, "More of them. Northward."

She saw the dust, followed it down to three riders coming at a steady lope. They seemed to be a good half mile distant. She and her vaqueros watched them approaching, eventually made them out as gringos, perhaps range men, at least they were dressed as range men. They had booted Winchesters under each saddle fender, something no range man carried during the course of an everyday horseback ride, or while working.

Hernan' leaned to speak softly to Anna Marie when the horsemen were much closer. "I don't know them. They're not from around here. They look like troublesome men, *señora*. Maybe we should move back a ways."

She replied without taking her eyes off the three heavily armed strangers. "We stay where we are. If they are friends of the people by the fire, we can face them all down at the same time."

Hernan' exchanged a look with José Elizondo and Gregorio Paredes. They were outnumbered, four to six, counting the three at the fire ring.

CHAPTER 2

No Trespassing!

The slightly hawk-featured man hunkering with his coffee at the fire saw the riders first, and put his cup aside as he unwound into a standing position.

The younger man and the girl also stood up. The older man said, "Friends of yours?" without taking his eyes off the advancing riders.

The younger man said nothing but the girl spoke. "They're the men who rode up to our camp day before yesterday. They —"

The younger man finished it for her. "They wanted my sister to ride to some town with a Mex name and go to dance with them. I think they ran off our horses. Anyway, we didn't mention this to you when you came along and helped us find our horses and brought us down here to your camp."

Hernan' brushed Anna Marie's sleeve but she spoke shortly to him. "Wait. You heard them."

18

"*Señora,* this isn't our trouble."

She put a withering gaze upon her range boss and spoke to him in Spanish. "Anything that happens on our land is our trouble."

The oncoming riders had seen the camp and had dropped down to a steady walk as they approached it. One was redheaded, another looked part Indian, but the man riding between his companions was graying and had a slit of a mouth. Two of them were bronzed from exposure. The half-breed was a softer shade of color but equally hard looking.

They reined to a halt a few yards from the stone ring. For a moment they studied the camp, their gazes lingering on the man with the graying temples who was with the young man and the girl.

The horseman in the middle said, "Cowboy, your visitors are goin' back with us."

Hernan', hidden in the underbrush, looked at Gregorio and José, then drew his six-gun. He had been right about one thing, these were troublesome strangers.

The mustanger answered softly and slowly, "Only if they want to, mister."

The mounted man answered quietly. "They'll want to. We got more to offer'n you have. Beans and coffee. We live good, cowboy." He looked at the youth and the girl, looked longest at her. "Get your horses," he

19

said in the same even, quiet tone of voice.

His redheaded companion dropped his right hand to the butt of his old Colt. His draw was a blur. He did not cock the weapon, he just smiled above it. "Get your horses," he repeated.

The mustanger eyed the man holding the gun and said, "Put it up, mister. No one's goin' anywhere unless they tell me they want to."

Instead of holstering his weapon the redheaded man swung it to bear on the mustanger.

Anna Marie stood up in plain sight out of the underbrush. At first only the mounted men saw her, then the girl and boy turned to stare. The mustanger did not take his eyes off the redheaded man.

Gregorio and José arose with Winchesters snug against their shoulders. When the mounted men did not turn back facing him the mustanger finally also looked atop the brushy swell. He seemed as surprised as the mounted men were.

Anna Marie ignored the men and spoke to the girl. "What is your name?"

"My name is Betsy, Elizabeth Conners. This is my brother, Chet."

Anna Marie continued to ignore the men. "Betsy, do you want to go with those men?"

"No, ma'am. I'm afraid of them."

Anna Marie put her stare upon the man with the lipless mouth. "Do you need any more of an answer than that?"

The mounted man's eyes narrowed when he replied. "Lady, whoever you are, this ain't none of your affair."

"Anything that happens on my land is my affair. Ride back the way you came and don't return."

Surprisingly the hard-looking horseman nodded, smiled in Anna Marie's direction, cast a final look at the people by the stone ring, muttered something to his companions, and did exactly as Anna Marie had said. He led off, riding northward.

No one moved until the three riders were out of shooting range. Finally, Anna Marie's vaqueros lowered their weapons and she stepped into full view as she said, "Saddle up. You'll ride back to the yard with us. Particularly the man who built that horse trap on my land."

The graying man did not move.

Anna Marie eyed him for a minute, then said to Hernan', "Shoot him."

Hernan' looked aghast.

Anna Marie did not take her eyes off the mustanger. "It is up to you, mister."

The mustanger smiled up at her. "Be right

with you," he said, and led Chet and Betsy out where their horses were hobbled. He spoke to them out there but the distance was too great for Anna Marie to hear what was said.

They led their horses back to the stone ring and rigged them out. As they started up the brushy slope Anna Marie and her riders went after their own horses. Both parties came together on the sundown side of the swell, Anna Marie erect in her saddle, Chet beside his sister, clearly bewildered, while the man with gray at the temples nodded for Anna Marie to lead out.

Gregorio and José rode on each side of the strangers, Winchesters across their laps. Anna Marie beckoned for Betsy to come up front with her.

They could have covered the distance to the yard in half the time if they had loped, but Anna Marie had set the gait, and it was a steady walk with reins swinging.

She told Betsy who she was and how they had happened to be atop the swell, and in turn the girl told her everything that had happened at their previous camp, and for many months before.

By the time they reached the yard Anna Marie had the sixteen-year-old girl smiling a little. She was very pretty, with dark violet eyes, even features, and a complexion like peaches and cream.

Anna Marie took the girl with her to the main house, leaving her riders to care for the animals and take the mustanger and Chet to the bunkhouse with them.

Evening came slowly this time of year. Sometimes it did not get dark until almost nine o'clock. Betsy Conners helped Anna Marie prepare their supper. They talked of many things. Anna Marie told the girl about her husband, about the ranch, and by the time they had finished supper and the darkness was broken only by lamplight from the main house and the bunkhouse, Anna Marie felt slightly uncomfortable; she hadn't talked so much in almost three years. Perhaps because she hadn't had much female companionship for that long. She had friends over in Hermasillo, about six miles away. Most of her friends were married women she visited occasionally, but never for long if their husbands were around. It had been a long and lonely time for her since Fred had died.

She showed Betsy to a room, then went out to sit on the veranda before retiring. Too many untoward things had happened too suddenly.

There was laughter at the bunkhouse. Anna Marie hadn't been part of very much laughter for a long time. Partly because she hadn't had time for it, partly because while she trusted and liked her hired riders, she remained their employer — a widow-woman in a country dominated by men.

Hernan' came to say he would bed their guests down at the bunkhouse. She asked about Betsy's brother and Hernan' told her, "They are orphans. They have been working wherever they could, which was not very often. The boy would not leave his sister, and she seemed to bring problems wherever they went."

"She's a very pretty girl, Hernan'."

"*Si*. Yes, she is."

"And the other one?"

"The mustanger? He said he knew something was bothering the other two when he came across their camp, and brought them down to his camp, hoping his company would help."

"It helped," Anna Marie said dryly. "The Lord knows what would have happened otherwise. Did either of them know those other three?"

"No, *señora,* they only met them day before yesterday. They told the girl and her brother they were cattle buyers visiting ranches to get enough cattle to make up a drive."

"This time of year, Hernan'?"

"Well, cattle buyers make up herds as they

travel along any time of year." Hernan' shifted his stance. "Is the girl all right?"

"Yes. Tell her brother I think she and he ought to stay here for a while, until we can be sure those cattle buyers have gone on."

Hernan' nodded and departed in the starbright but moonless night.

Anna Marie rocked and listened to crickets, to the far-distant song of roaming coyotes, and when she decided she would go back inside a stocky silhouette came around the side of the house and said, "Good evening, ma'am."

She was standing when he came to the steps leading to the veranda. "Good evening," she replied. "You'll be leaving in the morning?"

"Yes'm. Whatever trouble there was is past now."

Anna Marie nodded. "Tear down your horse trap, and if you ride east or west, or even north, don't set up another camp for thirty miles."

He did not climb the steps but stood looking up at her. In the starlight she looked as young as Betsy Conners. He cleared his throat. "Well, suppose I rode south?"

"Ten miles," Anna Marie answered.

"This is a pretty big outfit, ma'am."

"I'm not ma'am, I'm Anna Marie Miller."

"That sure is a pretty name. My name's Kenneth Castleton."

She nodded crisply. "Remember, Mr. Castleton: Ten miles south or thirty miles east and west."

She left him standing there, blew down the lamp mantles in the parlor, and headed for her bedroom.

He had intended to mention the three armed strangers but she did not give him a chance, so he went down to the barn to make sure his thoroughbred bay horse was grained and hayed, then went over to sit on the bunkhouse porch and roll a smoke.

The girl and the lad were in good hands now, better hands than he could have provided. He'd never been married but that hadn't interfered with his ability to admire handsome females, and this particular day he had encountered two, one soft and sweet and beautiful, the other one cold, disdainful, and curt.

He killed the smoke and went inside to unroll his blankets on an empty bunk and bed down.

In the morning he shook hands all around, bent to receive a kiss on the cheek when he met Betsy down in front of the barn as he was saddling, and although he looked toward the main house, saw no one over there, so he rode out of the yard in the direction of his horse trap.

It irked him to have to dismantle the trap. There was precious little timber down here in the grassland country, so he'd had to carry what he'd used to build the trap from the distant foothills. If he had known there was a town nearby he might have gone over there to replenish his supplies, but he hadn't known about Hermasillo any more than he'd known about the Miller home place, because although he'd scouted enough to have found abundant evidence of unshod horses, he had not traveled east more than a mile from his trap.

And when he finally saw them tanking up inside his trap at the spring, every horse had a two-letter brand on the left shoulder, the side every man would see as he mounted up. FM.

It was not unusual to mistake the unshod horse tracks of branded animals from wild horses. Stockmen pulled the shoes of the horses they turned out. After a month or two the best-trimmed hoof spread, cracked, and got veiny, like the hooves of mustangs who had never been shod.

He went to work in the afternoon tearing down his trap. He was in no hurry; in fact, dismantling something he had expended so much sweat and labor to construct went against his grain.

It was evening before he had half the poles

27

and stringers on the ground. He quit for the day and made a lonely supper at the stone ring. Once, he had been a top hand, knowledgeable about cattle, good with horses, and as accurate a roper as ever came down the pike. But that had been for other people. The last two years he had been trapping wild horses, and while it was anything but risk-free, at least he went pretty much where he wanted to go, did what he pretty much wanted to do, and didn't have to wait for Saturday night to have a little whiskey if he wanted to, which is what he did as he stirred his meal over a fiercely hot fire of dry manzanita, which burned down about as fast as a man could shove more twigs inside the stone ring. He had a couple of pulls from his bottle.

For this man born in a Montana hamlet called Monmouth, life hadn't been very easy. His parents had been killed in a snowslide when he was six years old. All he had as mementos was his father's big old stem-winder with the spidery hands under a glass that could be opened by pressing down on the winding stem, and a locket his father had carried on his gold watch chain with a tiny painting of his mother inside.

There had been a few good times but mostly it hadn't been something he wanted to remember, until he was big enough and handy enough to hire on with cattle outfits. Things changed gradually. He became a top hand, a genuine professional stockman, the kind of rider who was paid top wages.

But, as happened with many range riders, his restlessness arose less from a wanderlust than from a desire to try other things. Maybe there was the hope that somewhere down the line he would find something he could dedicate his life to. So far it hadn't happened. Trapping wild horses was a challenge. He enjoyed the freedom it gave him, but he had begun to feel over the last few years that mustanging wasn't it.

For one thing, mustanging was hard and dangerous work, which he did not object to, but neither was it very lucrative, and that, he had come to understand when he was crowding forty, was the measure of a man's success and achievement. Money.

In Ken Castleton's case he owned a good bay horse, a sturdy but worn Visalia saddle, a double Navajo saddle blanket, a service-able bridle, a bedroll, two guns, and very little else.

As he worked at tearing down his horse trap he considered — and rejected — a number of trades he could probably make a living at. He was a range man and a very good black-smith. Rarely did those two things come together for a man accustomed to open country and a degree of freedom. Blacksmiths had their shops in towns, and while every cattle outfit shod using horses, usually in a three-sided shed, cowboy blacksmiths were rarely accomplished shoers, and no ranch Ken Castleton had ever come across would hire someone just to shoe horses.

He paused at his labor to have another pull from his whiskey bottle. The result did not help his sense of futility but it seemed to make it at least temporarily more bearable.

He did not see or hear the solitary rider approaching from the east until his hobbled bay horse threw up his head and nickered. It was close to dusk.

By then the raw-boned, tall man with the expressionless face and the dull star on his vest was less than a hundred feet away.

Ken pitched his last stringer aside, put on his hat, and went to the stone ring. The raw-boned man with the tipped-down hat neither spoke nor nodded as he dismounted and led his horse to the opposite side of the stone ring. He had by then taken the measure of the man and his demolished horse trap. He finally said, "Most folks would ask around before they settled into a strange country, mister."

Ken could have agreed with that but didn't; the taller man's attitude was contemptuous and it rankled Ken a little. He did not reply, so the lawman smiled. It reminded Ken of a rattler's expression before it struck.

"What's your name, cowboy?" the lawman asked.

"Ken Castleton. What's yours?"

"Sheriff Walt Brown," the raw-boned man replied, still wearing a small humorless smile. "I reckon you run into Mrs. Miller, eh?"

Ken nodded — moccasin telegraph was exceptionally fast in the Conejo country.

"Well, Mr. Castleton, let me give you some advice. It ain't just the Miller outfit; all the land for a hunnert miles in all directions is deeded. None of the owners takes kindly to fellers like you. If I was in your boots, I'd saddle up and not even look back for three, four days."

That ended the visit. Sheriff Walt Brown turned his back to Castleton, swung up across leather, and gazed flintily downward for a moment before reining around and riding back the way he had come.

Ken had another pull on his bottle.

CHAPTER 3

A Clash of Wills

At one time Ken Castleton had owned a packhorse, but he'd lost him in some northern mountains and although he tried to track the thieves, there was too much pine-needle country, which made tracking next to impossible.

Now, as he rigged out the big bay, made his bedroll fast behind the cantle in the pale dawn of a new day, he had everything he otherwise owned in a pair of large cavalry saddlebags.

Going north, as everyone had suggested lately, seemed reasonable. He tanked up his horse at a little snow-water run-off creek where the water was cold enough to hurt a man's teeth, and kept on riding. He did as the sheriff had suggested: He did not look back.

He wondered a little about the orphaned lad and his pretty sister. He also thought about the handsome woman with ice water for blood.

In the early afternoon he scouted up a little

knoll near a creek for his night camp, hobbled the bay horse next to the watercourse, and unrolled his bedroll. He made a tiny cooking fire from dry deadfall limbs that gave off heat and no smoke, and was mixing the batter for hoecakes in the same skillet he would use to cook them, when he glanced down toward the creek where his horse had been cropping wild timothy.

The animal was standing like a statue, head up, little ears pointing. Ken arose from his supper fire, passed among the trees of his low knoll, and watched in all directions for movement.

When he saw them, watched their progress southward from up in the direction of some brushy and timbered foothills, he would have bet new money it was the same men who'd come to his camp a few days back.

Three men, riding on loose reins with sunlight reflecting off metal cheekpieces and the steel butt plates of booted rifles.

He hunkered in front of a rough-barked old tree and watched them approach several hundred yards west of his knoll, on their southward course.

Cattle buyers? Riding down across Miller ranch land armed to the teeth? Hard-looking men who had camped somewhere back in the foothills out of sight?

The three horsemen passed well west of his little hill. If he'd fed green wood into his cooking fire they could not have helped but notice smoke. He hadn't used any green wood — dry wood was best for a fast, short-burning fire. And it put off no smoke.

It did put off an aroma, but if the three riders picked it up, they passed along as though they hadn't.

He had to move among the pines atop his low knoll to keep them in sight. They were a long distance southward before he thought he saw another rider join them. They stopped, dismounted, and seemed to be palavering. They had halted near a stand of ancient, squatty white oak trees, which made it very difficult to make out details, but horses, in shade or sunlight, were large animals.

There *were* four of them.

Ken returned to his midday meal. Afterward he scoured his frypan with grass and put it away, rolled a smoke, and went back through the trees. The three riders were no longer in sight. They could have gone southward in one of two directions. Due south across open grassland, which would be the course most riders would have taken, or they could have passed into the oaks, which were abundantly shady, where they would not be seen.

In the far distance, evidently loping away

in a southeasterly direction, was the fourth rider. Ken killed his smoke and watched that one because there was nothing else moving as far as he could determine. He frowned, trying to pin down the notion in the back of his mind that the distant horseman was familiar, an unlikely thing since he had seen only Anna Marie Miller's vaqueros, the brother and sister orphans, and Anna Marie herself on horseback.

The identification arrived like a blow, although the rider was far too distant now to be certain. If it was that cold-acting sheriff . . . men didn't rendezvous secretly unless they had something to hide.

Ken watched the day die, the smoky dusk settle, heard birds making their soft perching sounds in the overhead trees, and went down to the creek to take an all-over bath. He remained down there as warm evening yielded to warm nightfall. His horse was dozing hipshot within hearing distance of the little creek.

Eventually, he returned to the knoll for supper and this time he draped his bedroll over his upturned saddle to prevent firelight from being seen southward.

After eating a meager meal and putting the utensils aside for morning use, he took two swallows from his bottle, rolled and lit a smoke, and settled comfortably with his back to a tree.

The advice Sheriff Brown had given him, along with the cold admonition from the handsome widow, weighed heavily in his thoughts.

He owed none of them anything. Except for the youth and his sister, everyone had made it very clear they did not want him in the Conejo country.

He smashed the cigarette into a bare place where there were no needles, arose, and went to stand on the knoll gazing southward.

He thought the three heavily armed men were capable of anything. He'd encountered their kind before in different places and under different circumstances. If they had not reappeared, had not obviously been camping on the outskirts of the Miller range instead of riding elsewhere seeking cattle to buy, and if they hadn't met that horseman, of whose identity Ken Castleton was almost certain, he could have rolled into his blankets with a clearer mind.

In the middle of the night his horse whinnied, awakening him instantly. He sat up and waited. The horse did not make another sound and without a moon he could not see the horse well enough to discern whether it was genuinely upset or not.

With a scorching curse he pulled on his

36

boots, took the Winchester leaning against a tree, and stalked out to the edge of the timber atop his knoll. There was not a sound for a long time, not until he was about to return to the opposite side of the knoll to find his horse, then it came distantly but unmistakably; the protesting bellow of driven cattle. He'd brought up the drag in enough cattle drives to know that sound.

He stood stiffly erect for seconds, then returned to finish dressing, buckle his cartridge belt and Colt into place, take his hat off the low snag of a nearby tree, and start down to where he'd left his saddle in tall grass not far from the horse.

That small, shrill voice in the back of his mind repeated what it had said earlier: This was none of his business.

But men driving cattle in the middle of a moonless night were unlikely to be doing it for a legitimate reason. As he was saddling and bridling the long-legged bay horse it also occurred to him that unless he was as incorrect as all hell, what he would find — if he found anything — was that it was the "cattle buyers."

The distant bawling dwindled. Ken made a guess that the drovers had let the cattle spread out along the little meandering waterway.

They would not let them tank up for long. If they were doing what he increasingly felt was a fact, the one thing they had to depend upon was time.

It was somewhere past midnight. Dawn would arrive somewhere between four and five o'clock in the morning. Unlike horses who could be run at high speed for several miles and cover a lot of ground if made to, cattle were not built for running, so rustlers had to know what they were doing when they made a cut of someone's cattle and drove them off. They had to have a knowledge of the ground, the habits of the stockmen from whom they'd stolen cattle, and have a destination that would shield them from detection after sunrise, if they were pursued. Not all rustlers were pursued; cattlemen had riders out every day, but with hundreds of cattle, very often the loss of thirty or forty head was not noticeable until long after pursuit or detection was possible.

If the rustling was discovered within hours of the time it had occurred and pursuit was undertaken, it was usually not too difficult to recover the cattle. If the thieves saw pursuit on their trail, they would leave the cattle and outrun anyone who was a mile or two back. If they escaped they could try again another day.

Ken's bay horse suddenly blundered into a prairie dog village of an acre or so, broke through with both front legs, and went down, throwing his rider on hard ground, half knocking the wind out of him.

The horse recovered first and stood with reins dangling, more confused and bewildered than frightened, which allowed Ken sufficient time to catch his breath, shake off dirt, and walk up to the horse.

Normally he would have cursed a blue streak. This time he was too occupied to do more than kneel and feel the horse for broken cannon bones. He straightened up, relieved that there was no serious injury, and brushed dirt off them both before he walked ahead of the animal, leading it safely through the mine field of hidden underground passageways.

It took half an hour. By then, strain as he did, he heard no cattle.

He squatted in the predawn chill and had a smoke. Then he arose to lead his horse back and forth, turning it sharply left and right in case it had strained shoulder muscles, which it evidently hadn't, tightened the cinch a little, swung back astraddle, and changed direction.

Even if he'd caught the rustlers, there would have been little he could do alone. Seasoned outlaws would almost certainly have someone riding back to watch their trail.

It was getting downright cold. He freed his

jacket from behind the cantle, shrugged into it, and without haste covered enough ground so that when false dawn appeared, he was within rifle shot of the Miller ranch yard.

There were lights at the bunkhouse and at the main house. He approached neither, but led his horse into the dark old barn, stalled him, forked him feed, and even purloined a coffee tin of rolled barley for him, before returning to the yard.

Hernan' Iturbide stopped in midstride and stared. Ken said, "Good morning, range boss," and the older man got his tongue loose from the top of his mouth to reply.

"Good morning. You should be thirty miles from here by now."

Ken eyed the light at the main house, took the *mayordomo* by the arm, and walked him across to the covered veranda where it was as dark as the inside of a boot, and released Hernan' only to rattle the door with his knuckles.

Anna Marie appeared in the doorway, fully attired as though ready to ride. Behind her somewhere two voices reached Ken, along with the smell of cooking and brewing coffee.

Anna Marie looked as stunned as Hernan' had looked. Before she could speak Ken pushed them both past the door into a large parlor furnished with heavy, carved dark furniture, and smiled as Betsy and Chet Conners came to the kitchen doorway to stare.

"Ma'am," he said to Anna Marie, "unless I'm very wrong you were raided last night."

For five seconds there was not a sound, then Hernan' muttered something in Spanish.

Ken told them his entire story from beginning to prairie dog village. When he'd finished Anna Marie was staring as though she was looking at a ghost.

Hernan' stood up and headed for the door. No one tried to prevent his departure. Anna Marie went to a chair and sat down with both hands lying in her lap like dying birds. "They drove them east?" she asked, and Ken wagged his head. "South, ma'am. A little east maybe, it was dark and I'm not familiar with the country, but it seemed to me they were going more south than east. What's over there, ma'am?"

"Hermasillo, our nearest town. About six miles from our yard."

Ken smiled without mirth. "Rustlers don't drive stolen cattle to towns, at least not that I've ever heard of. They avoid towns. How near are the closest railhead shipping corrals?"

Anna Marie arose and went to stand with her back to the smoke-darkened, big old stone fireplace in the south wall before answering Castleton.

"Forty miles south on the outskirts of a town called Shiloh."

Ken rolled and lit a smoke, went to lean on the wall nearest the front door as he spoke to her again. "In forty miles, if that's where they're heading, we could overtake them. Get a posse in Hermasillo and run them down. Even if they make the cattle hurry along, it'll be a long drive. Posse riders can cover the same distance in half the time."

Anna Marie looked past at the Connerses in her kitchen doorway. Chet pushed ahead. "I'll ride with you, Mrs. Miller." His sister took a couple of tentative steps forward, too, but before she could speak Ken Castleton addressed them both.

"You two stay here. Me'n the lady's vaqueros can do this, with a few posse riders an' that sour-faced sheriff from town."

Chet seemed ready to argue or protest but Anna Marie told them essentially the same thing Ken had. Then she added, looking imperiously at the mustanger leaning in her doorway, "And I'll ride with the posse."

He did not even hesitate. "Ma'am, you're not riding with any posse."

They traded hostile glances as she replied. "You're still on my land, Mr. Castleton."

He did something he had rarely done in front of women. He swore. "I don't give a damn if I'm trespassing at the gate of Heaven, ma'am, you are not going!"

She was going to respond when Hernan' entered and told her, "The men are ready. We have saddled a fresh horse for him." Hernan' jerked his head to indicate Ken Castleton.

Anna Marie Miller replied to her range boss in an inflectionless voice that dripped icicles. "Saddle my horse, too, Hernan'."

The dark foreman's eyes widened. He looked from the handsome woman to the mustanger, saw no help was going to come from that quarter, and spoke almost pleadingly as he said, "*Señora*, no. It cannot be done. This is man's work. It will be dangerous. We will return as quickly as we —"

"*Saddle my horse, Hernando!*"

She seldom called him Hernando. He cleared his throat and looked again at the mustanger. "*Señora, por favor.* No."

Anna Marie was erect and glaring. "Hernando, you've always done what you were told."

The *mayordomo* was crushing his hat to his chest. Ken Castleton straightened off the wall. "Saddle her horse, Hernan'." He was smiling straight at the handsome woman across the room when he said this. Hernan' yielded without another word and left the house.

Anna Marie's stony gaze returned to

Castleton. "Do you expect me to thank you? I don't need help with my riders."

Ken continued to smile, looked at Chet Conners, and walked slowly toward the fireplace. He stopped directly in front of her. "Ma'am —"

"If you call me ma'am one more time I'll have the vaqueros tie you backwards on your horse and turn him loose."

Chet and his sister were rooted. They'd never before seen such a fiery test of wills between a woman and a man.

Ken let several moments pass, then without warning seized Anna Marie in a powerful grip, spun her around and shoved her into Chet Conners's arms. "Boy, you can tie her to a chair, or you can lock her in a room, but if she comes out of this house before we're gone, I'll scalp you alive."

Chet clung to Anna Marie until the mustanger was gone, then freed her as she struggled against him.

She pushed the door, but it would not budge. The mustanger had cocked a porch chair beneath the knob. She turned around white-faced with blazing eyes and hurried to the rear doorway leading from the kitchen to the veranda.

The mounted men were already riding southward into the darkness. She went back indoors, put her back to the door, and glared at Chet Conners.

His sister broke into racking sobs. It was the only sound as the rattle of men riding away faded into silence outside.

Anna Marie ignored Chet as she went to Betsy and put both arms around her.

CHAPTER 4

The Trail

Hermasillo had a few lights showing but the main part of town was dark as Ken Castleton and the vaqueros arrived there. They routed out a livery barn night man, a youth in his teens who stood before the four riders blinking himself awake.

He recognized the vaqueros but the other man with them was a stranger to him.

Ken asked him where Sheriff Brown lived. The youth raised a skinny arm as he replied. "Yonder at the hotel, only I don't think he's up there. He rode out right after supper an' as far as I know he ain't come back. . . . Wait a minute, I'll see if his horse is in its stall."

The scrawny youth returned looking mildly chagrined. "Must have come in when I was dozin' in the harness room. His horse is in its stall."

Ken led up the north roadway as far as the ramshackle old wooden rooming house —

46

known locally as the hotel — tied up out in front, left the vaqueros there, and had to rattle a locked door several times before a potbellied older man carrying a lamp unlocked the door and glared.

Ken asked if the sheriff was in his room, and the proprietor, who had been roused from sleep, continued to glare as he said, "No, he ain't. He never come back after supper."

"You're sure?"

"Yes, dammit, I'm sure. Hasn't been no light under his door all night. . . . What is it — some drunk fall off his horse?"

Ken replied in a mollifying tone. "Sorry we got you up. Thanks an' good night."

The old man slammed the door with unnecessary force. The vaqueros laughed.

Ken stood looking for the saloon, but it was also dark, and padlocked. He looked for the jailhouse, but it too was dark.

Hernan' offered a suggestion, the result of visiting Hermasillo and listening to the gossip for many years. "There is one place he might be." Hernan' jutted his jaw toward the lower end of town. "A woman named Belinda Herman lives in one of those little houses. It has a red door." Hernan' shrugged and turned to snug up the cinch of his horse.

They rode down there and this time when Ken knocked on a door the woman who opened it was smiling. She was on the sun-down side of thirty, with carroty hair and a big mouth colored bright red. She looked from Ken to the vaqueros and gripped her wrapper tightly as she said, "Come back after breakfast, cowboy. And leave your friends behind."

Ken asked her the same question he had asked the potbellied man. The woman seemed indecisive for a moment before she said, "What is it? Is it important?"

"We need a posse," he told her, and after a moment of staring she said, "Just a minute," and closed the door. Behind Ken Castleton's back the vaqueros were grinning.

The man who opened the door had sleep-puffy eyes, tousled hair, a long nose, and a lipless mouth. He looked for a long moment at Ken Castleton, then started to swear. "I told you to get the hell out of the country. Do I have to hammer it into your skull?"

The vaqueros were no longer grinning and Ken's answer to Sheriff Brown made them stand a little straighter, the way men do when they scent trouble.

"You better have a very good hammer, Sheriff. Someone ran off some Miller cattle last night. We need some possemen to go after them with us."

The sheriff's expression changed. He hung fire before speaking again. "An' what's all this

48

to you? Never mind. You got any idea which way they went?"

"I think they went southeast. I started after them but my horse fell."

The sheriff ranged a long look out where the Miller riders were waiting, then gruffly said, "I'll get dressed. Meet me over at the jailhouse in a few minutes," and closed the door as Ken was turning away.

Hernan', Gregorio, and José started leading their mounts in the direction of the local jail. Ken Castleton walked behind them, head lowered in thought.

At the hitching post in front of the jailhouse the men looped their reins and leaned, looking up and down the only real thoroughfare Hermasillo had. Someone rolled and lighted a cigarette. Hernan' studied Castleton and decided it was not an auspicious moment for conversation, sighed and squinted in the direction of the carriage lamp burning brightly out front of the livery barn. In Hernan's opinion they were wasting time, and even granting stolen cattle could not be driven very fast, the rustlers already had several hours head start.

Hernan' was a philosophical individual. If they were meant to recover the cattle and apprehend the thieves, it would happen. If not, it would not happen. But even the most fatalistic person would have become impatient when, after a quarter of an hour, Sheriff Brown had not appeared.

Ken was leaning on the hitching post gazing in the direction of the cottage with the red door when Hernan' ventured an opinion.

"Companion, time passes. The thieves could be far on their way."

Ken nodded. "One of us should have watched the back door, Hernan'," and at the bewildered look this statement brought to the older man's face, Ken was about to speak again when Gregorio Paredes pointed southward.

Sheriff Brown was striding through the pre-dawn gloom. He reached the hitching post, looked at the waiting men, and said, "No posseman's going to leave a warm bed at this time of night, but I'll ride with you." He was turning away in the direction of the livery barn when he also said, "Can't see any damned tracks until it gets lighter."

At the livery barn, while the vaqueros waited, Ken followed the sheriff down the boardwalk, which was feebly lighted by a hanging lamp. No one had bothered to clean the mantle or trim the wick in ages, with the result that not only was the light poor but the lamp smoked.

There was no sign of that threadbare youth until Sheriff Brown went to the stuffy little unkempt saddle and harness room for his out-

50

fit. The youth was dead to the world atop a pile of sweat-stiff saddle blankets and was aroused only when the sheriff growled at him. The lad stared at the two men and would have risen but Ken said, "Go back to sleep."

Sheriff Brown dumped his outfit, led his horse out, and proceeded to cuff it from poll to fetlocks. Ken watched this with a dawning idea: Sheriff Brown was killing time.

This fit in well with what Ken had been pondering on his stroll from the house with the red door to the hitch rack in front of the jailhouse. It *had* been the lawman Ken had seen out yonder the evening before palavering with those so-called cattle buyers, who were most likely the cattle thieves.

Ken returned to the roadway where the vaqueros were waiting. Hernan' raised his eyebrows in a silent inquiry, and Ken smiled at him. "He'll be along." Hernan' appeared to accept that, but his impatient expression remained in place as he drew a pair of braided rawhide reins back and forth through his fingers.

The sheriff emerged from the barn astride his horse, and halted staring coldly at Ken Castleton. "Lead off," he said. "You're the feller who knows where they went."

It was not a very auspicious beginning. They had wasted more than an hour waiting for the lawman; there was to be no posse, and Ken had no idea where the rustlers were heading, except in a very general way. Briefly, back in Anna Marie Miller's parlor he had thought they had been driving the stolen cattle toward Hermasillo. Now, he thought they had probably crossed the stage road north of town somewhere.

He led off up through dark and silent Hermasillo in an increasingly chilly predawn by way of the north road. Even in poor light where the cattle had crossed the road there should be sign.

Sheriff Brown did not ride up with Ken, he remained back with the vaqueros, occasionally conversing with them in Spanish.

They were almost two miles north of Hermasillo when Hernan' wrinkled his nose, then rode up ahead of Ken leaning from the saddle. Ken's surmise was correct, where the cattle had crossed they had left abundant indication of their passage. Driving grass-fed cattle any distance, particularly in haste, induced them to leave an unmistakable trail.

The riders stopped as Hernan' gestured in the direction the drive had taken. They would have ridden in that direction but Sheriff Brown caused a delay by dismounting, loosening his cinch, and resetting his saddle. As he was cinching up again he said, "Y'know, gents, chasin' after outlaws in the dark's got a lot of men a place in a lot of cemeteries."

Hernan' looked in exasperation at Ken and raised his rein hand to continue riding, when Sheriff Brown also said, "Maybe you're right. Seems there was some cattle stole and drove this way." He paused long enough to mount and even up his reins before continuing. "An' maybe you was right back in town; we need a posse."

Ken Castleton's reply to that was short. "Go back an' round one up if you want, Sheriff. When you're ready to ride you can pick up our tracks and follow them."

Walt Brown put a cold stare upon the mustanger and said, "Go ahead, lead off."

It was evident that the sheriff was causing delays. When he remained back with the vaqueros as the chase continued, they either did not speak to him at all or made minimal replies when he tried to start conversations, something the sheriff eventually noticed, and he lapsed into a sullen silence.

With the first streaks of gray along the horizon, Hernan' rode ahead at a slow gait. It was easier now to follow tracks. He told Ken Castleton that his estimate of the number of cattle being driven was about a hundred head. He also said something that made Ken look closely at him.

"Last spring when we worked the cattle, there was a cranky old mottled cow with big horns. She was missing. I've known that cow for five years. She comes in every fall with every bone showing but with a sassy-fat big calf at her side. The *patrón* used to say he didn't want fat cows with runty calves. The best cows were those who came in bony with big calves. I knew that cow; she'd fight a man on horseback if she had a little calf. She was dangerous but her calves were among the best."

Ken asked if Hernan' had mentioned this to his *patrón*'s widow and the *mayordomo* shrugged. "Once, yes, but with so many cattle, she said maybe wolves had gotten her. I did not mention her again. But now I wonder; how many cattle have been stolen; how long has this been going on?"

Ken kept his thoughts to himself. When the sun arrived the trailing was much easier. In fact, Ken and Hernan' rode ahead, under the baleful stare of Sheriff Brown. Only when they came up atop a fairly high hill that offered an exceptionally good view of the countryside roundabout did Ken begin to have misgivings.

They could see for miles in all directions. There was not even any dust, let alone a sighting of moving cattle.

Hernan' rolled his eyes and muttered in

54

Spanish. Ken looked at him and the *mayor-domo* hastily repeated his comment in English. "They flew away. Look; not even any dust. They were maybe driven off by *fantasmas,* by ghosts. Maybe the phantoms had the power to make them invisible."

Ken said nothing as he dismounted, and rolled and lit a smoke. Those damned cattle and their drovers were out there somewhere. Maybe they were passing over rock now, something that raised no dust, but they were out there.

If it had recently rained there would be no dust, but Ken had been in this country for several months and there had been no rain.

He and Hernan' were squatting in horse shade atop the hill when the others arrived and dismounted. Sheriff Brown squinted, stood a long time with his back to the others, and eventually slowly turned and put an unfriendly gaze upon Castleton. "Where are they?" The sheriff made a sweeping gesture. "Nothin' showin' out there, mustanger. Where are they?"

The only answer was to mount up, and keep following the tracks. A mile farther along, when Hernan' rode up, Ken asked him if he was familiar with the country ahead. Hernan' shrugged; he had ridden over much of it at one time or another, but no, he could not say he knew it as well as he knew the Miller range.

Ken asked about ranches and Hernan' shook his head. If there were ranches farther south, they would be in country he did not know. He told Ken, with a strong stare, that the sheriff undoubtedly knew the country, and that maybe Ken should ask him.

They smiled bleakly at one another and continued to lead the others. Nothing was said between them about Hernan's suggestion.

Heat arrived, not as searingly as it would be later in the year, but hot enough to make everyone tie their coats behind their cantle.

Their horses needed water. When Ken spoke of this to Sheriff Brown he got a look of indifference. As far as Sheriff Brown was concerned, there was no water in the direction they were riding for another two days. That was at a Mexican hamlet whose name Brown did not remember. Otherwise, the sheriff told them, there was precious little water the farther they went, and what there was was jealously guarded by those who either owned the land or who controlled it.

The tracks showed stirred soil where foot-weary animals had passed along. The rustlers were no longer pushing the cattle but neither were they allowing them periods of rest. Under this kind of treatment cattle would "shrink," or lose weight, rapidly.

What particularly puzzled him was the relentless way the rustlers were continuing their drive into a waterless country where dense thickets of chaparral and mesquite seemed increasingly to dominate the land the farther south they rode.

He almost believed the thieves had not known the territory, but that made no sense.

No one would risk their lives stealing cattle only to drive them until they dropped. He told Hernan' he would ride ahead and left with the sun nearly overhead and bearing down.

It was more than a mile ahead when he crested a brushy rib of land running east and west that he thought he might have an answer, but the distance was too great to be certain. In a big volcanic depression sunshine reflected off what could be metal objects, and there was a clearly visible meandering wagon road leading from somewhere farther south into the big round depression.

When he eventually saw the others coming, they halted and did not continue their approach for a long time. Ken turned back to studying the distant depression and only looked around again when his companions finally arrived.

They had seen him atop the ridge and had picked their way carefully to his position. The first rider was Sheriff Brown. He dismounted stiffly, loosened the cinch of his horse and turned, finally, to look around. Ken pointed out the distant place that seemed to have metal objects, perhaps in a yard of a ranch, or at least in a place where there was or had been a ranch.

Hernan' and the other vaqueros crowded up and squinted into the dazzling sunlight. None of them said a word until the sheriff gestured eastward and said that was the direction the tracks were leading, and turned to snug up his cinch as though to mount up.

Hernan' seemed almost apologetic as he turned to mount and agreed with what the sheriff had said. Ken rode back down off the brushy ridge behind the others.

Where they picked up the tracks again they did in fact make a broad easterly trail, bearing a little southward but only on a long trail as though the men driving them had a destination in mind somewhere more to the south than to the east.

Gregorio Paredes, riding several hundred yards to the north, abruptly halted and waved his hat. He had found a sump spring.

As they watered the horses here but did not drink themselves, Hernan' stepped close to Ken and, speaking in a low tone, wondered aloud why the rustlers hadn't watered the cattle here. Ken's response was equally soft. "Because they were in a hurry — and my guess is that they had another place to tank them up."

Hernan' went over among the vaqueros as Sheriff Brown approached Ken looking sour. "Well," he said, "how far do you expect to go, cowboy? This is big country and it's mostly waterless, as you've seen. I got an idea it'll get drier the farther south we go, until us an' our horses will really suffer."

Ken smiled at the tall man with the bloodless lips. "It'll be as hard on the rustlers as it'll be on us, Sheriff, an' as near as I can figure out, they're not quitting."

Walt Brown turned and went over to his horse. All the animals were dripping water and beginning to feel a little better. They had been without feed since yesterday, they had been under hard use with not enough rest. Like men, horses, too, had limits.

When the men left the sump spring Hernan' rode ahead following the broad trail of driven cattle. They all had noticed shod-horse tracks among the imprints of cattle, but had not expected anything different. As Ken had said, there were three rustlers.

The sun shifted off center, a few weak shadows appeared on the far side of the increasingly thick, flourishing patches of infernally thorny underbrush, which in places rose higher than a mounted man.

Ken had encountered this kind of country before, but had never willingly made extensive sojourns through it. Even wild horses, to whom any kind of feed was acceptable, would have given a very wide berth to the land he and his companions were now traversing.

CHAPTER 5

Reasons for Despair

It was a long hour before they rode up the easterly rim above that old abandoned ranch down in the big depression and halted.

"There they are," Ken Castleton said.

The cattle were lounging around a stone trough that leaked water at both ends. There was no sign of the rustlers, but there were several buildings in the process of decay where they could have put their horses and settled in to rest.

Sheriff Brown wagged his head and pointed in the direction of a dust cloud moving in from the distant north-south stage road.

Ken eyed the dust for a moment and made his worst decision thus far. He said, "Find a way down, Hernan'. If that's the rustlers returning we want to be down in the yard before they get here."

Hernan' had little difficulty finding a trail from the rim downward. Behind the others Sheriff Brown picked his way and with the

61

riders in front watching the footing, he drew his six-gun and tossed it into a thicket.

In places the downward trail was rocky and treacherous, but it obviously was still in use because the wiry brush on both sides had been unable to reclaim it. Hernan' was out front riding straight in the saddle with both feet barely in the stirrups, the way a man rode who wanted to be prepared if his horse fell.

When Hernan' was within a hundred yards of level ground, the cattle must have seen them and a few cows became spooked. These animals ducked their heads, snorted softly, and rolled their eyes as though ready to run, which they would have done except that the other cattle did not move.

Hernan' remained in the lead after flat ground had been reached, his narrowed gaze fixed upon the cattle. He was too distant to see the brands but he didn't have to see them, he recognized several of the cattle.

Ken looked back where the sheriff was slouching along, looked ahead where that dust banner was getting closer, and told Hernan' to head for the large barn with warped siding and a sagging roof.

The cattle moved a little as the horsemen passed by them, but did not offer to flee as they watched the riders head for the old barn. They were foot-sore and tired, otherwise they probably would have scattered.

Everyone dismounted out front and led their horses inside the barn. Like everything else in this place, it smelled of musty abandonment, but at one time it had undoubtedly been the pride of someone. It was large and wide with clear evidence that at one time it had been used. Wild pigeons flew out the doorless rear opening as the men led their horses inside.

Ken asked Sheriff Brown who had lived here and why they had left. The sheriff only shrugged, keeping his right side turned away as he flipped up a stirrup leather and loosened his cinch. There was only one trough, out where the cattle were milling. If they'd led their horses over there to water them, the cattle would probably run. No one offered to water the horses, they had something more critical in mind — those oncoming riders they were convinced would be the rustlers.

Ken and Hernan' went out back in barn shade to watch the dust, but now it was possible to make out the men beneath the dust. Hernan' sucked in a quick breath. "Six," he said, standing very erect for a moment, until his companion spoke.

"The three we tracked here had friends. Or maybe they already got the cattle sold and the new owners are coming to take delivery."

63

Whoever the riders were was not as important to the range boss as their numbers. In his view it did not matter who the riders were, there would be a fight if they tried to take the cattle. He said, "We better scatter among the old buildings, not all of us be in the barn."

Ken considered this and contradicted it. "If we're all in the barn they wouldn't be able to get at us one at a time."

Hernan' shrugged. The oncoming horsemen were too close now for anyone to risk running toward the other buildings.

Sheriff Brown strolled out back, watched the approaching horsemen, and said, "It's too many to be the fellers we been following. We better let them get in here before we do anything."

Ken turned, the sheriff was standing half-turned so that his right side was not visible, which at the time Ken did not think about.

Hernan' hurried back up through the cool and gloomy interior of the barn to tell the vaqueros there was to be no action until the riders were in the yard.

A few minutes later six hard-riding men entered the yard, hauled down in sliding halts, and Hernan' caught his breath and stood rooted. He knew most of those men.

Ken came forward and the *mayordomo*

caught him by the arm. Before Hernan' could speak Sheriff Brown strolled to the front and stepped out into plain sight. Ken was too surprised to heed the restraining hand on his arm.

Sheriff Brown called to the six riders. "In the barn. Them three I knew would be doin' it, and another one, a mustanger Miz' Miller and me run out of the country."

Ken started forward but Hernan's grip tightened as he said, "The man on the sorrel horse is Hermasillo's town blacksmith. The men behind him is the harness maker. That one wiping his forehead owns the saloon."

Ken remained still until the strangers dismounted and started toward the barn. He pulled free of Hernan's restraining hand, walked up nearer the front barn opening as Sheriff Brown faced slowly around wearing a malevolent smile as he addressed the heavily armed men standing out there with him. He gestured. "There's the cattle. The rustlers is inside." He touched his empty hip holster. "They took me captive in town, took my gun an' made me ride with them."

Not a sound came from the men in the barn, but the Hermasillo blacksmith, a powerfully muscled man with a trimmed beard and testy eyes, told the men he had arrived with, "Three of you go 'round back." As this order was being obeyed the blacksmith pushed past Sheriff Brown and stopped just short of entering the barn. He could see armed men in there, with Ken Castleton closest. They exchanged stares before the blacksmith gave his ultimatum. "Get rid of your guns, or use 'em. If you use 'em we're goin' to leave you down here for the buzzards to pick on."

There was no acceptable alternative, the men in the barn dropped their weapons, and three men entered the barn from out back as the blacksmith led his other companions inside from out front.

Ken came to a slow realization of what had happened, but it did not at this time make sense to him. The blacksmith went over Ken for other weapons as his men did the same to the vaqueros. José Elizondo had a boot knife, which one of the riders held up for others to see before he contemptuously hurled it against the wall, swung José around, and shoved him so hard he nearly fell.

With the worst moment over, the blacksmith handed Ken Castleton's six-gun to Sheriff Brown, which he briefly examined before dropping it into his empty holster.

The saloonkeeper looked steadily at Hernan' Iturbide, whom he had known for years, gave his head a disgusted wag, and growled for the vaqueros to walk out of the barn.

The blacksmith addressed the sheriff. "What about the cattle? Push them ahead on the way back?"

Brown's answer was curt. "She can come after her damned cattle." He laughed. "First she's got to find more riders. Let's head back with this carrion so's I can lock 'em up before dark."

They would not reach Hermasillo before dark but all the blacksmith said was, "Damned good thing Belinda didn't waste no time. As it turned out, we just barely got here in time."

Sheriff Brown went after his horse while the men from Hermasillo led the other animals out, got their prisoners mounted, and used piggin' strings to make each man's wrists fast to his saddle horn.

Thus far none of the prisoners had said much, and even as they were leaving the yard only Gregorio Paredes asked for a smoke.

The rider rolled one, leaned to place it between Gregorio's lips, and lit it. He had not said a word. But as he straightened up in the saddle he said, almost reproachfully, "Hell, if she didn't pay you enough, you could have rode on, you didn't have to rustle cattle."

Gregorio rolled his good eye skyward as he deeply inhaled, exhaled, and said nothing.

They did not return to the stage road, which was a couple of miles due west. That would take too much time. Every one of the riders from town had a business to run. They rode on a northwesterly course that would cut miles off the otherwise long return trip. Sheriff Brown and the blacksmith rode up ahead in desultory conversation. Ken watched them, especially the lawman. He still could not figure out why Sheriff Brown had gone to all this trouble to make it appear that Ken and Anna Marie's riders were cattle rustlers, but he had no difficulty in understanding, now, why the sheriff had caused all those little delays even after leaving town. He had to slow the pursuit of rustlers as long as possible in order for those townsmen to get down to the old abandoned ranch.

There was another mystery, but Ken did not think about it until daylight was waning and they could barely make out town roofs up ahead. The real cattle rustlers had not been at the ranch. He assumed they had seen men coming down that treacherous trail from the eastward rim, and had hightailed it.

When they entered Hermasillo very few people were abroad. The raggedy-pantsed youth at the livery barn stared as the townsmen rode off toward their homes and left Sheriff Brown to untie his prisoners, tell the youth to look after the horses, and herd the prisoners in the direction of the jailhouse.

The lawman steered his prisoners to benches, then lighted the office lamp and hung it back on its ceiling hook. Of course the news would spread like wildfire; this kind of news always did, but there would be no curious people appearing at the jailhouse until morning, and only the very brash ones would appear then.

Sheriff Brown fired up his little potbellied iron stove and shook the coffeepot to be sure it wasn't empty before going to his desk to sit down, lean forward, clasp both hands, and gaze at the silent men opposite him.

The prisoners stared at him until Ken said, "It was too well planned, Sheriff. You killed damned near an hour here in town, and on the way down yonder you used every trick to hold us back. You knew those riders were coming. Most likely you got that carroty-headed woman to roust them out after tellin' us you wouldn't be able to get up a posse in the middle of the night. None of that bothers me as much as why you did it."

Sheriff Brown's expression did not change as he looked at Castleton. He said, "What the hell are you talkin' about?" He smiled at Ken. "Try convincing those fellers who brought you back that you fellers didn't run off the cattle from the Miller place, make me go with you so's there'd be no lawman in town, an' make the mistake of lettin' me get free for a few minutes to get the woman to slip around and tell them what you'd done. Try makin' 'em believe otherwise. You're a saddle tramp, them Messicans most likely been schemin' ever since Miz Miller's husband died. When you-all come together you went into the rustlin' business. Let me tell you something, cowboy, hereabouts they got no use for rustlers or horse thieves." The sheriff arose and growled for his prisoners to walk ahead of him into the cell room. After he had locked them in, the vaqueros in the same cell, Ken Castleton in the cell opposite them, he turned back toward the office without another glance or word.

The moment they heard the cell room door slam, Hernan' spoke in a hushed voice to the man in the opposite cell.

"I still can't believe it." Hernan' made a gesture with both arms. "It was deliberate?"

Ken sat on the edge of the wall bunk and did not look up as he replied. "It happened. We're in here, aren't we?"

Gregorio and José came forward to join the conversation. The man with the wandering eye said, "*Jefe*, I don't understand."

Ken looked up for the first time and bleakly smiled as he told the vaquero he did not understand either. He felt the lumpy corn husk mattress, stretched out on the bunk, and closed his eyes. There was no point telling them right now that he was sure the sheriff had met with the thieves before they rustled the cattle.

When he awakened someone was noisily pushing metal food trays under the doors. Without moving Ken watched the sheriff complete his chore and look past the bars at the vaqueros. "Next time you plan a raid, don't let a damned greenhorn help you," he growled, and turned away.

Not a word was said until the door between the cells and Sheriff Brown's office had been slammed, then the rider with the wandering eye looked upward, flung his arms wide, and shook his head. What had happened and what was evidently still happening was too much for the vaquero. He went back to sit on a bunk, making no move to take one of the food trays.

Across from him Ken ate everything on the tray and was still hungry; coffee would have alleviated this condition but the sheriff brought none.

The vaqueros spoke among themselves in Spanish. Ken lay back on the bunk with both hands beneath his head trying to make sense out of what had happened. It intrigued him that Sheriff Brown was still acting as though he had rustlers in his cells when he knew damned well he didn't have, but one thing he would have bet his wages on, if he'd been earning any, was that Sheriff Brown knew exactly what he was doing.

While events were still vivid in his memory he went back over them episode by episode. The probable reason the rustlers had not been seen leaving the old ranch was because Ken and his companions had been entirely occupied with watching where they were going on that treacherous trail from the rim to flat ground. If the rustlers had seen them coming, they would have fled — but not westward where they would have been seen, and not northward. . . . Ken's eyes widened. If they had fled westward they would have encountered the riders from town.

They had to have fled southward or perhaps eastward.

Ken sat up on the bunk, and rolled and lit a smoke. He decided they had gone eastward, perhaps around the circular rim of the dry meadow where the ranch had been.

He smoked the cigarette down to a nubbin, dropped it on the stone-hard earthen floor, and stared at the opposite wall. It had been too perfect an escape, almost as though the rustlers had simply abandoned the stolen cattle, possibly even before that dust banner approaching from the west had been visible in the yard of the abandoned ranch.

He paced the cell, was watched by the bewildered and subdued vaqueros across the narrow passageway, and when he abruptly halted scowling at the wall, Hernan' called to him.

"What is it?"

Ken went to the steel bars and while gripping one in each hand, said, "The whole damned thing was planned even before we went after them. Hernan', we did exactly as someone figured we'd do, and rode into a trap like fools."

Hernan' nodded. He, too, had been going back a little at a time. "And what happens to us now? I can tell you, because I've seen it done in Hermasillo. They lynch rustlers and horse thieves."

Ken's reply was short. "We get the hell out of here." The vaqueros gazed at Ken as though he were crazy, and one of them said a little plaintively, "How?"

Ken did not answer because he had no answer. He returned to perch on the edge of the bunk and roll another smoke.

A light chill came into the jailhouse. Each cell had a high, very narrow slit of a window with two steel bars embedded in the opening although no one over seven years of age could have squeezed through, and maybe not even then.

Ken considered their immediate situation. Maybe the Miller riders knew people in Hermasillo, but he didn't, and the people who had known the vaqueros for years would undoubtedly be hostile once the sheriff's version of what had happened had circulated.

Ken lay back on the bunk, pulled the threadbare old tan army blanket over himself, and tried to sleep.

CHAPTER 6

An Unusual Day

Anna Marie was still angry when she took the two orphans to the corral with her to saddle three horses. Not only was she upset with the mustanger's treatment of her, but she was furious at the way Hernan' Iturbide had disobeyed her. He had never done that before, and now, as the three of them rigged out in silence, she decided it must have been the mustanger who had influenced her *mayordomo*.

Not until the three of them were riding southwesterly under a vaguely overcast sky and Chet Conners said, "Ma'am, they was right; runnin rustlers down isn't anything a lady had ought to do," did her mood seem to lighten a little.

She eyed the tall youth, saw the way his sister was watching her, and forced a smile. "Maybe not, but those were my cattle."

Betsy interrupted to point out a golden-breasted bird singing its heart out in the grass. Anna Marie identified the creature for her.

"Meadowlark. They nest in the grass. I've seen them rise up and fly in the face of a cow they think might trample their eggs."

The morning was cool, the sun hung behind them as they rode. Whenever they encountered small bands of FM cattle Anna Marie would stop to make a saddle-back appraisal, and except that most of the animals were skittish, they appeared fine, or, as Chet Conners observed, "Slicker'n moles."

Anna Marie asked the youth if he'd worked cattle. He nodded. "For maybe three years, off an' on, different places."

"You didn't stay in one place very long?"

The boy shook his head. "Drifted, Miz Miller. My sister'n I kept looking."

"For what?"

The brother and sister exchanged a look. "Our folks was killed in a runaway when we was younger. They used to tell us about a place called South Pass. They owned land up there an' ran cattle. Not a big outfit like you got, but the way they talked about it, they loved the country."

"And you were trying to get back there?"

"Something like that, Miz Miller."

"Isn't South Pass up in Wyoming?"

"Yes'm."

"And you're down in New Mexico?"

Betsy picked up the conversation when

her brother seemed to hesitate. "We met a real nice old man in Colorado who said he'd take us in through the winter. He had a nice ranch. We went with him."

Her brother sounded harsh when he interrupted to say, "It was a long winter, Miz Miller, an' he never quit pesterin' my sister. Finally, just short of spring I come onto them in the barn. He was holding my sister and the harder she struggled the madder he got, until she upped and slapped him. He stepped back with his fist cocked when I come up behind him. . . ."

It was clear that Chet did not want to continue. She said softly, "I'd like it if you two would stay with me." At the look she got from them both, she also said, "I'm going to need another rider, Chet. I pay top wages and expect top work. Betsy . . . I need another woman on the place. I'm tired of seeing men everywhere I look."

Neither Chet nor his sister spoke until they'd come close to a bosk of ancient oaks that had been one of Anna Marie's favorite places for years, and she led them into deep shade to dismount and admire the view. Then Chet said, "I'd be proud to hire on, Miz Miller, an' you'll get your money's worth."

He did not look at Anna Marie, he looked at his sister. She was smiling.

With that settled, Anna Marie wondered aloud how far her vaqueros had had to go to find the stolen cattle, and since neither of her companions knew the country well enough to comment, neither of them said anything. Not until Chet made an offhand remark that most of the FM cattle must be farther off because all they'd seen so far, and they'd covered quite a bit of ground, were little bands of maybe fifteen or twenty head.

Anna Marie explained that this time of year the cattle would usually range up north closer to the foothills where there were springs and abundant feed. When they had rested long enough she led off in that direction in an easy amble. It was a fair distance, she did not expect to have to cover all of it. There were knolls and, in some places, hills from the top of which it was possible to see for many miles.

The hillock they eventually came to had a few trees atop it, and evidence that someone had recently camped there. As Anna Marie sat her saddle looking at the campsite, she said, "This must be as far as he got the first night. He should have gotten farther."

Betsy said, "Who?"

Anna Marie's gaze swung to the girl, showing the smokey stare of hostility. "The horse trapper."

"Mr. Castleton?"

Anna Marie's resentment was too deep for her to mention the name, so she merely nodded, then turned her horse to scan the uneven, somewhat scrubby country that gradually, on a northward slant, became mountainous, wild, and timbered uplands, a rugged, unspoiled wilderness.

Cattle did not go into country like that, not voluntarily anyway, because pine needles soured ground where no grass grew. Also because the smell of cougars and bear was strong. Anna Marie dismounted and stood at the head of her horse with the reins dangling from one gloved hand. She was frowning faintly.

Behind her the brother and sister also swung to the ground. Chet stood a long while studying the vast flow of westerly and easterly run of grassland, and said as though speaking to himself, "Where are they?"

Anna Marie turned. "I don't know. Every other time I've come up this far they've been out there, scattered but in sight." She turned to look toward the forbidding, dark uplands and Chet said, "Not up there, Miz Miller."

She nodded absently and turned to mount her horse.

They left the knoll riding west with the primitive high country on their right, and saw shod-horse tracks that seemed to be heading southward, but there was nothing down there but the same range they had recently traversed, except for a straggling stand of white oaks to the west. Chet paid them scant attention; like Anna Marie he was seeking signs of cattle.

The only livestock they encountered was a pair of wet cows watching them from a thicket, their calves standing close to their mothers.

Chet saw the troubled expression on Anna Marie's face and said, "This time of year, most places I've worked, cattle drift closer to the home place."

Her answer to that was that in the places he had worked farther north, cattle could sense changes of season sooner. In this part of New Mexico, cattle did not drift toward a winter feeding ground because cattle grazed year-round, except during those very rare occasions when heavy snow fell.

They spent the better part of the afternoon looking for cattle. What had started out as a pleasant horseback ride turned into a day-long hunt for cattle. They only turned homeward when Anna Marie had to give up because dusk was approaching.

Very little was said on the ride back. When they entered the yard and dismounted to care for their animals, Chet ventured a remark. "You got a lot of land, Miz Miller, an' if there's one thing I've learned, it's that cattle are mostly not where folks expect them to be."

Anna Marie said nothing. She and Betsy went in the main house to light lamps and start supper. Without Chet they discussed the failure to find cattle. Betsy, who knew only what she had picked up from her brother, wondered aloud if he hadn't been right about livestock rarely being where they were supposed to be in open range country.

Anna Marie's answer to that was simply that she'd lived all her married life on the Miller ranch, and not once in all those years had there been less than a few hundred head on the grasslands they had ridden over.

She also said, with a hint of wistfulness in her voice, that she and her husband had gone up there in a buggy with a picnic hamper of food, and had stopped west of the knoll they had ascended today, over where there was a trout stream, and she had cooked what he had caught.

Betsy was young, but she had a woman's intuitive knowledge of when to speak in a situation like this, and when not to. She busied herself setting the big round kitchen table with the gingham-patterned oilcloth atop it.

It was dark before Chet arrived, scrubbed, his hair slicked down, and hungry as a bear cub.

Anna Marie had had very few supper guests since the death of her husband, they had invariably been neighbors, older people who enjoyed a whiskey and water before eating. This night, although she went to the liquor cupboard, she did not open it.

They were halfway through a solemn meal when a rider came into the yard from the west, tied up in front of the barn, and crossed to the main house to knock at the door.

His name was Amos Daggett. He had cattle several miles to the east, closer to Hermasillo. He was a sturdy, stocky man, graying and weathered. He and Frederick Miller had been close friends as well as neighbors. They had used their crews to help one another work cattle. Amos Daggett was one of the cowmen who had wagged their heads about Frederick Miller's widow being able to hold things together after her husband's death.

When Anna Marie opened the door, recognized Amos, and invited him in, Amos remained outside with his hat in one hand as he said, "Walt Brown's got your riders an' another feller in his jailhouse."

Anna Marie's surprised expression encouraged the cowman to tell her the rest of it. "Seems them vaqueros of yours an' this other feller run off about a hundred head of your cattle, an' got caught somewhere down south by Walt Brown an' some riders from town."

Anna Marie stepped out and closed the door at her back. She was silent so long that Amos Daggett put on his hat and was turning away when she finally spoke. "This stranger, did he have graying hair at the temples, was about medium height with — ?"

"I never saw him, or your riders, Anna. I just heard the talk in town. Folks are fired up. It don't matter whose cattle get rustled, they don't like it. . . . I got to get back, I figured you'd be out here all alone, wonderin' where your riders were."

She thanked him, watched him go down, mount up, and ride back the way he had come. She knew his wife, who would be worrying about his long absence at suppertime.

She went to a chair, sank down, and stared out across the quiet yard northward. It was impossible; Hernan', José, and Gregorio would never have stolen cattle from her.

About the mustanger she was less certain.

This may have been the reason she had found so few cattle up near the foothills. The longer she mulled over what Amos Daggett had told her, the more her antagonism toward the wild-horse hunter grew. She still could not believe her vaqueros would have done such a thing; they'd been fiercely loyal to her husband, and after his death they had seemed equally loyal to her. If there was any truth in it, she told herself, the mustanger must be responsible, but she still had trouble believing Hernan' and the other vaqueros would have done such a thing, regardless of how persuasive the mustanger might have been.

She was still out there on the porch when Chet came out, looked at her in the shadowy gloom, and went to perch on the railing as he said, "Somebody you know, Miz Miller?"

She told him everything that had been said and after a long moment of quiet, he gently shook his head. "I don't know about your riders, but Mr. Castleton didn't come across to me as a rustler."

She flared at him. "What do you know about him? Only that he rescued you and Betsy from those men who were after her. For all you know, Chet, he may have had the same idea in mind those strangers had. Betsy is a beautiful girl."

He nodded about her last sentence. "Yes'm, an' that's mostly what's kept us moving. It happened on cattle outfits, in towns, even sometimes on the road. . . . But I'll stake my saddle that Mr. Castleton isn't no rustler. Miz Miller, he wouldn't have taken your riders and rode all night looking for your cattle. If he'd been a rustler he wouldn't have wanted your riders to do that, would he?"

Anna Marie was silent for a long time, staring out into the night. She eventually said, "Chet, you're young. When you're older you won't be so quick to form an attachment to someone you think has helped you."

He did not argue, but the expression on his face showed plainly even by feeble starlight that what she had said about Ken Castleton had not influenced him at all.

Betsy came out. Anna Marie told her what she had told her brother and Betsy went to a chair, sank down, and with hands tightly clasped, said nothing. Like her brother she would believe nothing bad about the mustanger, but unlike him, she did not always express her opinion.

Anna Marie arose. Chet and Betsy also stood up. Anna Marie looked at the lovely girl and softened. "Well, sitting out here until it gets cold isn't going to help any, is it? I'll help you with the dishes, Betsy."

"I've already done them, ma'am."

Anna Marie said, "Honey, please don't call me ma'am. I never could stand that. It sounds like someone very old."

Betsy smiled a little. "Miz Miller?"

"Well, yes, I suppose so. For the time being, anyway. Now, we'd better get a good night's sleep. Good night."

They watched her go back inside before

Betsy looked at her brother. "It's not true, is it, Chet?"

His reply was short. "Naw, not Mr. Castleton. Her riders I don't know, but they been on the ranch a long time. If they'd wanted to steal her cattle, what with her husband bein' dead several years and all, why would they wait until now? Something's wrong, Betsy. Mr. Castleton's no rustler."

Betsy accepted that because she had relied on her brother's judgment most of her life and he'd rarely been wrong; never where men were concerned.

She went back to the house and her brother returned to the bunkhouse, which still smelled of chili and coffee.

None of them slept well. Anna Marie's inclination to lay all the blame on the mustanger kept her angry until almost midnight. Betsy slept the best of them all; she had been troubled about the accusation that Ken Castleton was a cattle thief, but she went to sleep before either her brother or Anna Marie did because she had the wonderful conviction that no matter what it was, in the end everything would turn out right — in this case she knew in her young heart that the mustanger would be vindicated. She did not dwell for long on Anna Marie's dislike of the mustanger. That was something she could do nothing about.

Her brother bedded down in the silent, dark bunkhouse wondering why Anna Marie Miller hated the mustanger so much. He hadn't really done anything to harm her, and he had torn down his trap and ridden away when she had ordered him to.

He fell asleep while speculating about the difference between men and women. Why would an otherwise pleasant, at times understanding, very pretty woman like Anna Marie Miller take such an immediate and violent dislike to a man she did not really know?

CHAPTER 7

Hermasillo

In the morning Anna Marie said she would ride into town and verify what Amos Daggett had told her last night. Chet said he would ride with her. She thought he should stay with his sister but he shook his head, and one thing Anna Marie was learning about young Conners was that he was as stubborn as a Missouri mule. She still would have insisted on making the ride alone except that Betsy, perhaps recognizing Anna Marie's expression, quickly said, "I'll be fine," and removed a big-bore under-and-over derringer from a pocket. "I can use it, Miz Miller. Chet showed me lots of times." Anna Marie looked at the formidable small gun in Betsy's hand. "It was one of a pair we found at the bottom of an old trunk after we buried our folks." Betsy put it back in the pocket of her skirt.

Chet went to hold the door for Anna Marie and as she nodded her appreciation she noticed the beginning of a hard-set expression to his face which would, inevitably, become more pronounced as he got older.

At the barn he saddled both their animals, led them out front to be mounted, and smiled at Anna Marie. His smile was as honest and warm as the smile of a small child. She smiled back.

Betsy waved to them as they left the yard and they both waved back. With four miles to go, they talked, with Anna Marie asking questions a man would not have asked, but Chet did not seem to mind. In fact, like Anna Marie, he appeared to enjoy having someone to talk to about his and his sister's past life.

By the time they had Hermasillo in sight he displayed for Anna Marie's benefit the few sentences in Spanish he had learned at the bunkhouse. His accent was terrible, but she did not smile, she encouraged him to learn more.

It was, she told him, the second language of the Southwest, in some places the first language.

They rode down Main Street side by side and inevitably the gossip mongers saw them and hastened to tell others what they had seen.

A few people waved and Anna Marie smiled and waved back. The only thing Chet noticed about these encounters was that the people who had waved were all women.

At the jailhouse they had to wait for Sheriff Brown, but not very long, he had been up at the pool hall and had seen them pass.

When he walked in he smiled, took Anna Marie's hand, and held it a little longer than was customary, then sat at his desk, and without waiting to be asked, told her the story he had been telling since arriving back in Hermasillo with his prisoners.

She scowled faintly. "Not Hernan', Sheriff. I can't believe it of Gregorio or José, either. My husband hired them seven or eight years ago. They are as loyal —"

"Miz Miller, the facts speak for themselves. If you want I'll take you around town an' you can talk to the fellers who come down there from town. Your riders was in the barn with that mustanger. The cattle was out there actin' a little sore-footed from bein' drove so hard over rough country. They got quite a shrink on them."

"Sheriff — why?"

Walt Brown eased back in his chair looking slightly patronizingly at her. "All I can do is guess, Miz Miller," he said softly. "That old abandoned ranch where he caught 'em is isolated. My guess is that they'd made a deal with a buyer down there somewhere and agreed to deliver the cattle to that old ranch. Them fellers from town come in the nick of time. . . . That mustanger caught me here in town and took away my six-gun. He made me ride with them."

"Why would he do that, Sheriff?"

"Well, most likely with the sheriff not around, folks in town wouldn't know whether to go after them fellers or not."

"Sheriff, how would anyone here in town know I'd been raided? It was in the middle of the night, wasn't it?"

Walt Brown reddened, cleared his throat, and offered Anna Marie and Chet some coffee. They both declined and the sheriff's smile this time was less certain than it had been.

"Miz Miller, you know how gossip gets around. Faster'n lightning."

Anna Marie smoothed her riding skirt, removed her doeskin gloves, and stood up to fold them under and over her belt. "I'd like to see Hernan'," she said, and waited until the sheriff heaved up out of his chair. As he approached the locked cell room door he asked if she would like to talk to the mustanger, too. Anna Marie vehemently shook her head, something Sheriff Brown approved of.

Hernan' looked every year of his age, he hadn't been able to shave or wash. Neither had his two cell mates. When Anna Marie appeared all three of them broke into wide smiles and came to grip the bars.

Instead of speaking to her riders she said to the lawman, "Thank you, Sheriff. I'd like to talk to them alone."

For a moment it did not appear that the sheriff was going to depart, but he eventually did, offering one warning before he strode back toward his office. "Miz Miller, they're goin' to lie in their teeth. It comes as natural to men like that as breathin' does to decent folk."

Hernan' told her essentially the same story he and Ken Castleton had discussed. She listened with a deepening frown until he was finished, then avoided Chet's gaze, which was one of I-told-you-so, and asked about the hour her riders and the mustanger had reached Hermasillo. Hernan's answer made her appear more troubled than ever. Hernan' jutted his jaw in the direction of the opposite cell where the mustanger was leaning on the bars listening. "Ask him," Hernan' said.

Anna Marie turned slowly, her gaze as cold as ever, but her bafflement was greater than her dislike. She said, "You agree with Hernan'?"

The mustanger smiled directly at her. "Every word — ma'am," he replied, clearly willing to return her hostility. "We didn't take the sheriff's gun. And we didn't force him to go with us. By any chance, do you know a woman named Belinda Herman?"

Anna Marie's brow cleared, her gaze became fixed. In a town no larger than Hermasillo a woman like Belinda Herman was known.

"That's where he was when we found him, ma'am. He killed half an hour getting dressed and over in front of the jailhouse where we were waiting. He caused one delay after another on our pursuit so's someone here in town could roust up the riders who came down there, and when the sheriff told them we were the rustlers, they brought us back tied to our saddle horns. That woman with the carroty hair was told as sure as you're standing there to round up those riders and send them south. Ma'am, if they weren't told to ride south, why did they pick that direction?

"Go talk to the woman with the carroty hair. She can tell you about all you got to know — if she will."

Chet stepped close to the bars. "Mr. Castleton —"

"Boy, call me Ken."

"Yes sir, well, Ken, Miz Miller'n my sister'n me went riding yesterday." As he was speaking Chet pushed one hand through the bars with his back to Anna Marie and the vaqueros listening and watching across the narrow corridor. Anna Marie had to move slightly

93

to see the mustanger's face. It was expressionless, his eyes fixed on young Conners, who went on speaking.

"She took us up to the foothills where she said her cattle usually grazed this time of year. . . . There wasn't no cattle."

For a matter of seconds there was complete silence, then as Chet stepped back Anna Marie stepped forward. Castleton looked at her. She nodded. "We found a few spooky cows."

"How many head was usually up there this time of year?"

"Several hundred."

Ken's eyes widened. When next he spoke it had nothing to do with what she and Chet had told him. "Go see that Belinda. In case you don't know where she lives, it's in a small house at the lower end of town with a red door."

She said, "And if she verifies what you've said?"

"Go home, ma'am, and wait."

She stared at him. "Wait?"

"Yes, wait!"

She had ignored being addressed by the term she hated, although she understood perfectly why he had used that term. He was taunting her, the result of her own hostility toward him.

He scowled at her. "Go, dammit."

Chet nudged her. The pair of them returned

to the office where the sheriff was waiting. He looked closely at them both as he said, "Lies, Miz Miller. Whatever they told you."

She nodded and without another word to Sheriff Brown left the jailhouse, stopped outside to look at Chet. He smiled at her.

Walt Brown stood at his front office window watching them cross toward the general store where everyone in the community got their mail, and turned back to get himself a cup of coffee and stand with his back to the little stove as he sipped.

He stood like that for a long time going over things in his mind, otherwise he might have seen Anna Marie and Chet leave the store, walking toward the lower end of Hermasillo.

Belinda Herman had been washing her hair out back when they came around there. She picked up a towel, wrapped it around her head, and made an uncertain smile. She knew who Anna Marie Miller was, everyone in the countryside knew Anna Marie. But she had never been this close to the other woman and seemed uncomfortable as she forced a smile and said, "Good day to you, Miz Miller."

Anna Marie did not smile back. "Good morning to you, Miss Herman. Can we talk here or would you prefer going inside?"

"Talk about what? We can do it out here.

I haven't had a chance to clean house for a while. What is it?"

"Some men came to your house looking for Sheriff Brown . . ."

Belinda nodded, beginning to look either puzzled or apprehensive.

"And before the sheriff left to go with those men, he told you to go see someone. Who was it?"

Belinda Herman's apprehension increased. "We just talked is all."

"Once more, Miss Herman, who did he tell you to go see?"

"I don't see that it's any of your business what folks discuss."

Anna Marie's icy stare was unwavering. She allowed a long moment to pass before speaking again. "If the womenfolk of Hermasillo go before the town council and demand that you be run out of town . . . say, fifty women, Miss Herman . . ."

"You can't threaten me, Miz Miller."

Anna Marie shook her head very slightly. "I'm not threatening you. I'm giving you a promise. Regardless of what it costs, I'll spend the money to see you run out of town. For the last time, who did you go see after Sheriff Brown left your house?"

Belinda Herman raised both hands to press the towel closer to her head and wiped away

96

a trickle of water before answering. "Will Clavenger."

"The town blacksmith?"

"Yes. I was to tell Mr. Clavenger to get up a posse and ride south on the stage road until he came to a place where two big trees grow on opposite sides of the road, and to take the lefthand side road. That there was rustlers down there with a herd of stolen cattle."

Anna Marie said, "Thank you, Miss Herman," and led the way back around the house to the plank walk and did not even look at Chet until they were back where they'd left their horses. Then she said, "All right. We'll go home and wait, although I can't imagine what the mustanger has in mind."

Chet smiled slightly as they turned down a side street on their way back to the ranch.

Anna Marie was too preoccupied to make conversation until they were within sight of the FM yard, then all she said was, "That man goes out of his way to antagonize me."

Chet did not ask her to identify "that man" because he did not need a name.

Betsy came down to the barn to meet them. She and Anna Marie returned to the main house, leaving Chet to care for the horses. Once there, she dropped into a parlor chair and told Betsy everything that had happened in town, but did not tell her what her private thoughts had been on the ride back.

Anna Marie probably could have guessed what the girl would say if she'd been thinking about it. "We told you he wasn't a cattle thief."

Anna Marie gazed at Betsy and her heart lightened. Betsy could have been her daughter if she'd had children. She had developed a soft, warm spot in her heart for the girl.

Anna Marie went to the kitchen cupboard where the liquor was stored, poured herself a drink of whiskey and branch water, and returned with it to the parlor. Betsy showed nothing in her face as the older woman sat and sipped, but she had never before seen Anna Marie drink. It was a shock. She had seen men drink, but not women.

They prepared a meal and Betsy called her brother from the porch. He was out in front of the barn leaning on the hitching post staring in the direction of Hermasillo, and roused himself with an effort and crossed the yard.

Anna Marie was pleasant at their meal, as though she did not want to depress Betsy and her brother, but occasionally when they looked at her, the older woman's expression was solemn and troubled.

Later, when Chet and his sister could be alone down near the barn, he told her the parts of their Hermasillo visit Anna Marie had skipped over. He also told her something else and she blanched. "Why did you do it?" she asked in a slightly breathless voice. "Chet, that sheriff will come after you."

He studied the ground as he replied. "Because he isn't no rustler, and no matter what Miz Miller thinks, he did us a good turn an' we owed him that much."

Betsy studied her brother's face. "She won't want us around if she finds out, and if the sheriff comes out here, she'll find out. Chet, you put us square in the middle of something that's not really any of our business. . . . I don't want to have to leave."

Chet tried to comfort his sister but the longer they were together down by the barn the more distraught she became until he finally took her by both arms and said, "Don't you say a word to her, Betsy. Please."

She had tears in her eyes as she flared back at her brother. "How long have we been going from pillar to post? I haven't believed in a long time we'd ever get back to South Pass. And she took us in. She gave us a job and she treats me better'n I've ever been treated. You've ruined it all, Chet."

He released his hold of her arms and scowled. "Just let things take their course, Betsy, and don't say a word about any of this to Miz Miller. Everything takes time; this-here thing will take time. . . . Please?"

She nodded with tears, turned, and hurried back to the main house.

Anna Marie was in her husband's office when Betsy fled past toward her room. The older woman started to arise from the desk, then eased back down. What now seemed ages ago she too had been Betsy's age, not quite a woman and no longer a girl, self-conscious, doubtful of herself, easily upset and likely to cry for no apparent reason.

Anna Marie went back to work for a while, until she heard the sobs subside, then tiptoed down to look in past the open door. Betsy was sound asleep, her face red from tears. Anna Marie smiled softly. She remembered. In the morning Betsy would be normal again — whatever normal was.

She went out to the porch in the still, starbright night and sat in her rocker with con-fused thoughts. The mustanger hated her as much as she hated him, and that made her uncomfortable.

She thought of her husband, a man whose emotions rarely surfaced, strong, direct, yet soft and gentle with his wife. She had missed him but right now she missed him the most.

He wouldn't have sat on the porch knowing his cattle had been stolen. He'd have taken weapons, the riders, and never let up until he overtook the thieves. He had never told her so, but she knew that when he'd caught horse or cattle thieves he had either hanged or shot them. His world had been a simple place of right and wrong, black and white. He would never have done as she was doing, sitting out there rocking, doing exactly as the mustanger had told her to do — waiting.

By the time there was a chill in the air she saw Chet's light blink out at the bunkhouse, and arose to go inside.

Before going to her own room she looked in on Betsy again. She had awakened sometime, put on her nightclothes, and was now sleeping soundly, an expression of wonder and innocence on her face.

Anna Marie's heart ached for the child. She had so much to go through until she reached Anna Marie's age, and quite a bit of it would be heart-wrenching.

There were scurrying coyotes far out, their wailing cry softened by distance, a belated moon shone through her bedroom window to make shapes and silhouettes on the far wall exactly as it had done many nights since she had come to the Conejo country. What had once been mysterious and strange was now as much a part of her existence as eating and drinking, except for the diminishing although

101

not quite forgotten good times when her husband had been alive.

She was dozing off when she thought of Sheriff Brown, with whom her husband had always got along very well. But Walt Brown had become something her husband would have had trouble believing, without Anna Marie quite being able to figure it out or completely understand it, although she had begun to have some serious bad thoughts about the sheriff earlier, on her ride back with Chet from Hermasillo.

CHAPTER 8

Chet

For Walt Brown the sense of crisis arrived when Belinda Herman arrived slightly breathless at the jailhouse. He listened to everything she had to say, told her he would be unable to come to her house that night, and after she had departed he went up to the saloon, had two jolts, and went over to the café for several flat metal trays of food for his prisoners. On the way back across the road, he decided he had to do something he'd come close to in his life, but had never actually done — commit murder.

It did not bother him that it would be a woman: He had practically no regard for women. The main thrust of his thoughts dealt with what now appeared to be a desperate need for a diversion.

He was still preoccupied when he knelt in front of the cell containing the Miller ranch riders and pushed three trays under the door.

Behind him across the narrow corridor

103

someone cocked a gun. There were a number of sounds a man never forgot, but none caused a man's heart to skip several beats like the cocking of a gun.

Without moving, Sheriff Brown slowly raised his eyes. Hernan', Gregorio, and José were as stiff as logs staring over the sheriff's head.

Castleton did not raise his voice as he said, "Real slow an' careful, Sheriff, lift out your gun and push it under the door, too. Real slow, now."

Walt Brown obeyed very slowly, his color fading slightly. At the distance separating him from the mustanger a blind man could not miss.

"Stand up, Sheriff, slow. Stand up and turn around."

As the lawman obeyed Hernan' leaned to pick up the gun that had been pushed beneath his cell door. He held it without cocking it.

Walt Brown stared from the big-bore little belly-gun, cocked fully back and aimed at his middle. A rush of color came into his face. That damned Miller woman!

"Unlock my door," Castleton said in the same quiet manner. Sheriff Brown did not move, he was too angry at Anna Marie Miller for sneaking the little gun in to his prisoner.

"Unlock it, Sheriff, or I'll blow your guts out."

Walt stepped over, inserted the key, and twisted it. Castleton gave him another order. "Now do the same across the way."

Hernan' did not leave his cell when the door had been opened. Sheriff Brown turned back toward the mustanger. "That goddamned woman. I'll have her hide for this," he exclaimed, and Castleton shook his head as he stepped out into the corridor. "She didn't do it. Next time you lock someone up, make them take off their boots. . . . Hernan', put the son of a bitch in your cell and let's get the hell out of here."

Hernan' hesitated. "He'll yell and they'll hear him all over town."

"Gag him. Tie his hands and ankles, too."

All three vaqueros joined in this task and finally Gregorio and José smiled. They left the sheriff trussed and went up to his office, armed themselves properly, and followed Ken out the back door into an empty, dusty alley.

When they appeared in the livery barn the proprietor was up at the pool hall and his astonished scarecrow of a youthful hostler stared as though he'd seen four ghosts. He said nothing as four horses were led out and saddled. Not until they were leading the horses out back to be mounted and Ken tossed the dayman a silver cartwheel did the youth find his tongue. "Thanks, mister. Thanks a lot."

He went as far as the rear barn door and watched them leave town heading west. He was in the harness room an hour later when the liveryman came in, saw the ragged youth staring at the silver coin, and said, "Where'd you get that?"

"That feller Sheriff Brown locked up along with them Miller ranch vaqueros give it to me."

The liveryman seemed not to breathe for a moment. "In here, in my barn?"

"Yes, sir. They left out of here headin' west."

The liveryman lurched around with a squawk and went to the jailhouse. The town blacksmith saw him running up the opposite boardwalk and yelled at him, "What's got into you?"

The liveryman was panting from unaccustomed exertion and waved his hand for the blacksmith to come along without explaining.

By the time they had removed the gag so that the sheriff could turn the air blue with profanity, and untied his arms and ankles, a solid hour had passed.

He bawled at them. The burly blacksmith herded the liveryman ahead of him back down to the barn, where he passed an order that the lawman's horse was to be saddled, and one for himself, then he rushed up through town to recruit possemen.

It was late in the afternoon when six riders left town behind the sheriff. He was calculatingly deadly. He did not know the extent of the mustanger's knowledge about the stolen cattle, but he knew the mustanger, too, had to be suspicious.

Cattle were slow travelers. To get far enough away so that there would be considerable distance between them and their home range took a lot of time. In fact, if cattle could be driven six or eight miles a day, it was very good time.

What Sheriff Brown needed was time. He loped most of the distance to the FM yard and arrived there shortly before dusk.

Chet had seen a band of horsemen coming and had told Anna Marie. He was with her on the porch when the possemen rode in. Sheriff Brown saw her over there and did not nod as he dismounted and told his possemen to stay with the horses by the barn.

This time there was little civility between Sheriff Brown and Frederick Miller's widow. He did not go up to the porch but stood below it as he said, "Your riders show up, did they?"

Anna Marie's surprise was genuine. "My riders? . . ."

"Yes, ma'am, your damned Messicans an' that mustanger."

Chet started to speak and Sheriff Brown snarled him into silence. "Shut up an' stay out of this. Anna Marie, sneakin' that gun to Castleton makes you liable to arrest and jailing."

She continued to stare. "What gun? I didn't sneak a gun . . ." Her voice trailed off but she did not look at Chet while she was remembering how he had blocked her view of the mustanger for a moment.

"That damned little under-and-over forty-four caliber. You know what gun. Now, you tell me where they are or I'll haul you back to town, lock you up, and toss the key into the stove."

The blacksmith looped his reins and started in the direction of the main house. He was frowning when he got up beside the sheriff and said, "No call to talk like that to Miz Miller, Walt."

Brown whirled. "No call! She snuck a gun to the damned rustler, otherwise they'd never have been able to bust out. In all my time as sheriff I've never had no one break out of the jailhouse!"

The bull-built, dark-eyed blacksmith looked up at Anna Marie. He didn't say anything, he just looked at her with a disillusioned expression. As he was turning away Anna Marie said, "Mr. Clavenger, I did not sneak a gun into the jailhouse and give it to Ken Castleton!"

Clavenger turned back. "Then who did? How'd a gun get snuck to Castleton unless you done it?"

Anna Marie grasped at straws. "The sheriff isn't always in the jailhouse, is he? Anyone could have gone in."

The blacksmith slowly shook his dead. "Ma'am, except for you, us fellers who run him down, and the sheriff, don't no one in town know the man."

Anna Marie's surprise was past. She looked from the blacksmith to the sheriff and spoke quietly. "There is something I don't believe you know, Mr. Clavenger. When I was in town I talked to a —"

"Lies," bellowed Sheriff Brown. "Damned lies from sunup to sunset. Come on, Will, we'll search the ranch, an' if they aren't here, we'll make a manhunt. Come along."

The blacksmith turned his back on the people on the veranda and trooped back to the other waiting possemen with the sheriff.

Anna Marie did not say a word until she and Chet were inside in the parlor, then she turned on him. "Did you get that derringer from your sister?"

He answered without flinching or lowering his eyes. "No. It was the other one. We found a pair of them in Paw's old trunk. I made Betsy take one an' learn to use it —"

"And you had the other one when we went to town."

"Yes'm."

Anna Marie threw up her hands as Betsy came into the room from the rear of the house. She had heard loud talking. She looked from her brother to Anna Marie, put a hand to her mouth, and scuttled back the way she had come, tears flowing.

Six searchers could go through buildings and peer into lofts within a fairly short period of time, and the men with Sheriff Brown went about their search with considerable zeal. They had all heard Walt Brown's version of what had happened, and perhaps because they already believed what he had said about the men they'd brought back to town with their wrists lashed to saddle horns, they went about rummaging the FM buildings with thoroughness, right up until they met in front of the barn and the town blacksmith scowlingly asked Walt Brown if they hadn't ought to search the main house too. Since they'd found no one elsewhere it was the blacksmith's opinion that if the vaqueros and the mustanger were here, they would have to be at the main house.

The blacksmith appeared to be willing to pursue the hunt even though he did not like the idea because he and the Widow Miller's husband had been friends.

Sheriff Brown stood gazing in the direction of the main house. He did not believe the fugitives were over there, in fact after he'd ascertained that there were no recently ridden horses in either the barn or the corral, he had come to the conclusion that the wanted men were not on the ranch.

One of the other possemen rolled and fired up a smoke. He was a man of slightly less than average height with a thick neck and powerful torso. He, too, looked in the direction of the main house and spoke while trickling smoke. "They ain't here an' I don't think they come here, otherwise there'd have been sign, an' there wasn't none."

"Then where?" the blacksmith growled, and got no answer.

Anna Marie appeared on the veranda across the yard. She stood a moment without speaking, then she said, "Are you satisfied, Mr. Brown? They're not here and we have not seen them since we saw them in your cell room."

The sheriff did not respond. His companions followed his example and when Sheriff Brown led off out of the yard, neither he nor his possemen looked back.

Chet came out to stand beside Anna Marie. As he watched the men heading back the way they had come, he said, "If it's all right with you, Miz Miller, I'll saddle up and go back up yonder where the cattle was, pick up the trail, and follow it. Rustlers wouldn't head up through those mountains, they'd lose two-thirds of the cattle if they tried it. That leaves east or west. They sure as hell wouldn't come back down southward, would they?"

She was still watching the lawman and his riders when she replied. "Wait until morning, Chet, and I'll go with you. It'll be dark by the time you get up there now." She smiled at him, seeming to suggest that she had forgiven him for slipping the gun to Ken Castleton that had enabled the sheriff's prisoners to escape.

After she returned to the house Chet continued to stand on the veranda for a while, then went down to the barn to do the chores.

Dusk arrived gradually. Chet fired up the lamp in the bunkhouse and someone over at the main house did the same in the kitchen and in the parlor.

Betsy summoned her brother to supper. The meal was eaten in silence until Betsy asked Mrs. Miller where Mr. Castleton and the vaqueros would be if they had not returned to the ranch.

Anna Marie looked up quickly and said, "I think it depends on whether they really want to stay in Thunder Valley."

Betsy looked quizzical. "Thunder Valley?"

"That's the name of the big bowl the ranch is situated in. My husband told me it was the name the Indians gave it because during thunder storms, the sounds seemed loudest in the bowl."

Chet finished his meal and ignored the story of Thunder Valley to respond to what Anna Marie had implied earlier. "You know neither Mr. Castleton nor your riders was rustlers. By now that's real plain. If they didn't come back here it was most likely to keep you from gettin' more involved, an' maybe because they knew a posse would come here lookin' for them."

Anna Marie was raising her coffee cup when she smiled across the table. "You won't give up, will you?"

Chet's response was almost curt. "You don't believe they stole cattle."

"Don't I?"

"That's why you scairt the whey out of that woman with the sort of orange hair. After what she said in front of us both, you couldn't believe Mr. Castleton and your riders stole cattle from you. An' when you asked the sheriff in his office how folks would know you'd

113

been raided when it happened after they was abed, you saw the look on his face."

Anna Marie emptied her cup and set it down slowly. "Chet, what do *you* think?" she asked quietly.

His reply was louder, it matched the fire in his eyes. "I think the sheriff's either in with the rustlers or sure as the devil knows a lot more about what's goin' on than he should, him being a lawman."

Anna Marie smiled. She could have agreed. Instead she looked at Betsy. "Are you finished, honey?"

Betsy nodded, arose, and helped Anna Marie clear the table.

Chet went out to the veranda. He was still roiled. In his private heart he could not understand Anna Marie. She had to have arrived at pretty much the same opinions he held, yet she always seemed at the very last moment to hang back, to shy away from making any vocal commitments.

He went down to the bunkhouse, buckled his old cartridge belt and holstered Colt into place, took his Winchester, and went down to the barn by using the rear door of the bunkhouse so as not to be seen.

He brought a big stout using horse into the dark barn, saddled him, buckled the carbine boot into place, and led the horse out back

114

before mounting him.

There was a moon, not quite full but getting there, and there were millions of stars. The overcast of earlier in the week was no longer in sight, at night, anyway, but by daylight it was visible to the northeast as a great bank of dense clouds just beyond Thunder Valley's curving bulwark of mountains.

Later, Anna Marie and Betsy came out to the veranda, saw the light in the bunkhouse, and sat down as Betsy apologized for her brother's frankness. Anna Marie smiled at her in the gloom. "That's the only kind of a person you can trust, Betsy, the ones who say exactly how they feel and what they think." At the girl's doubting look Anna Marie patted her arm. "Wait, you'll see whether I'm right or not in a few years."

They discussed many things, but lingered longest over the rustled cattle, and when Anna Marie said that Castleton's last words to her at the jailhouse were "Go home and wait," Betsy looked puzzled.

"Wait for what?"

"I don't know. I could guess but I'm more inclined not to."

"Miz Miller — why do you hate him so much?"

Anna Marie smoothed her skirt before replying. She had a ready answer but refrained

115

from offering it. Instead, she said, "He doesn't like me."

Betsy said something that made Anna Marie's eyes widen. "He *does* like you. He teases, that's his nature. He teased me, I teased him back, and we'd laugh. I know he likes you."

"He didn't say so?"

"No, but he didn't have to." Betsy arose. "I think I'll go down and tell my brother good night. I'll be right back."

Anna Marie watched the girl striding in the direction of the bunkhouse, but her thoughts were elsewhere. Why didn't she like Ken Castleton? Trespassing? Building a wild-horse trap without finding out whether he was on private land? Because he called her ma'am when she'd made it clear she did not like being called that?

Betsy appeared on the bunkhouse porch as a soft silhouette. She was looking toward Anna Marie. "He's gone," she called.

Anna Marie stood up.

"Miz Miller, his guns and saddlebags are gone."

Anna Marie felt a hot surge of anger, let it subside as she went down to Betsy, and they both went to the barn. Chet Conners's saddle was not in its place on the saddle pole.

Anna Marie stared at the empty place. She

was angry with herself. She should have suspected he'd do something like this from the way he'd spoken at supper.

Betsy came up close. "Where would he go?" she asked.

Anna Marie knew where he had gone. "He'll be back," she said soothingly, but Betsy replied with the one statement Anna Marie could not counter.

"With his guns?"

Anna Marie put her arm around the girl's shoulders. "There's nothing we can do until morning, Betsy. By then he may be back."

They walked slowly toward the veranda as Betsy said, "He shouldn't have gone out there alone after the cattle. They'll kill him, Miz Miller."

CHAPTER 9

Toward Dawn

Daylight was waning when Ken and the vaqueros got far enough northwest to be in the foothill country.

Hernan' explained about the Miller ranch's custom of leaving the cattle up near the foothills where feed and water remained good until after the first frost, which, in ordinary years, did not arrive until the middle of November.

Moving several hundred head of cattle was not something that could be accomplished without leaving abundant sign, nor could it be done in haste.

By the time Gregorio, riding ahead of the others, located the trail and the others rode down to where he was, daylight was fading fast. Ken asked where the nearest water would be and José pointed in the same direction the cattle had gone. "Two miles, maybe. A good creek with fish in it."

Ken led off and the vaqueros, who had anticipated making camp, exchanged looks of resignation.

The farther west they went the more clear was the trail even in diminishing daylight. As before, when they'd hunted down the other stolen cattle, they hadn't required hoofprints, they could do fairly well by scent and droppings.

When they finally had to stop they were west of the creek José had mentioned near boulder country. Here, because the cattle had seemed to split out and around the rough footing, and it was possible there had been a deliberate division of the herd, they had to camp in order not to trace the route of one division and miss the other one altogether.

Their animals welcomed the hobbles, they were hungry, tired, and thirsty. Hernan' made a tiny fire that they concealed by placing their saddles around it. Supper was boiled jerky. Fortunately, jerky was already cured, and in fact they probably would have done just as well without trying to cook it. But the night turned chilly against the darkly timbered uplands to the north, earlier than it would have if they'd been farther away from the mountains, so anything that was warming was welcome.

They had not ridden hard, but rather steadily, since leaving Hermasillo, and they had ducked into a deep arroyo in the late afternoon watching six riders heading for the Miller yard.

They had already discussed the facts, and their suspicions were unanimous in what they had concluded, and except for being out-numbered, might have made a run on the six horsemen from town. Ken Castleton would have bet his outfit that if Sheriff Brown weren't the leader of the cattle thieves, he was certainly one of them.

Hernan' and the vaqueros agreed, having heard enough on the ride north to be influenced toward that decision mainly because of what they had suffered after being brought back to Hermasillo tied to their saddles, and also after hearing the complete fabrication Sheriff Brown had spread.

They were not as convinced that, if they recovered the FM cattle, surviving rustlers would implicate the sheriff. If that occurred they would be pleased. If it did not happen and they could recover the cattle, they would feel vindicated, particularly if they could catch the thieves.

None of them worried much about finding the cattle. Recovering them might be difficult. That would depend on how many rustlers were driving them, but, as Hernan' said while chewing a particularly tough piece of jerky, they might have an advantage if they did not allow the rustlers to see them.

The horses were out a fair distance, visible in the night only as large moving shapes. The men unrolled the blankets behind their cantles and prepared to bed down. It had been a long and somewhat disconcerting day.

José slowly straightened. He pointed to the horses. Each animal was erect, facing south-easterly. Because it was too dark to notice it, they missed seeing that several horses had un-chewed grass protruding from their mouths, but their stance was clear evidence even in poor light that something was approaching from below their camp.

Gregorio whispered, "Maybe they know we're back here. Maybe they've come back to kill us."

Hernan' did not respond. They could see nothing. There was no sound, either.

Ken Castleton spoke softly. "Fan out a ways. Whoever it is, they'll come toward our saddles."

Gregorio went south through tall grass and stopped often. The others scattered in different directions and also tried to detect sound.

For a long time, perhaps as much as fifteen minutes, there was only the silence of the long night, then Ken heard it: A horse, only one, coming up-country on a slightly northwesterly course.

He was at a loss except for a fleeting notion that it might be Anna Marie Miller. He discarded that, though after only barely considering it. Even if she was coming, she would not be doing so alone, she would have brought Chet with her.

The rider eventually was close enough for the men flat in the grass with guns in their fists to distinguish that he was neither a *fantasma* nor a skulker. They did not recognize him until he halted near their saddles and sat like a statue.

Ken Castleton almost swore in relief as he arose from the grass and called over there. "What in the hell are you riding around in the dark for? You could have got yourself killed."

The vaqueros also arose. All of them approached the rider, who had dismounted and was standing beside his horse. Hernan' smiled as he put up his handgun.

Chet nodded at Hernan' without returning his smile. Ken Castleton was not smiling. Neither were José nor Gregorio.

Ken said, "Is something wrong at the home place?"

Chet sank to the ground by the cooling embers before replying. "Well, no, but Sheriff

Brown came by looking for you fellers. He had a posse with him. They searched the buildings. The reason I come hunting you was because unless I miss my guess, Mr. Castleton, him an' his posse riders will be scourin' the countryside for you, an the odds is pretty bad. I figured, if I could find you, one more hand might be welcome."

They all squatted by the dying fire. The idea of Walt Brown hunting them with a big posse was, at the very least, unsettling. José quietly said, "Come daylight, everything will be different. If he's behind us and the rustlers in front of us . . ." José shrugged thick shoulders.

Ken gazed into the pink coals for a moment. The others, having become accustomed to relying on his judgment, sat and waited. Hernan' rolled and lighted a cigarillo. José became occupied with fiercely scratching inside his shirtfront and Gregorio's good eye remained fixed on Ken until Castleton said, "Well, gents. We can find the cattle come daylight. Might take a little riding, but we can do it. . . . What bothers me is that the sheriff will sure as hell eventually figure out the reason he couldn't find us was because we're on the trail of the cattle thieves. José's right, we can't have 'em behind us and in front, too."

Ken picked a crawling tick off his neck before continuing. "Either way, we're goin' to be outnumbered. Seems to me we got to take out the sheriff and his posse."

Hernan' stopped smoking and stared. "Kill them from ambush?" He seemed horrified at the idea. If it had only been Walt Brown he would not have batted an eye, but if the sheriff had townsmen riding with him in any numbers, regardless of how other things might eventually be resolved, folks would never forgive a massacre.

Ken grinned. "No, set them afoot."

Hernan' resumed puffing. The others smiled in approval until Chet asked how they would find the posse in the dark. He had no idea where they might be. The last he'd seen of them they had been riding in the direction of Hermasillo.

Ken's reply was brisk. "Sheriff Brown's involved up to his gullet. Remember how he delayed us on the ride south, how he killed time in town? His objective was to slow us down until the rustlers reached that abandoned ranch. My guess is that he had two reasons for acting that way. One was to give the riders from town time enough to get down there and catch us, which they did. The other reason was to give those riders who stole the cattle time to get plumb clear, and that worked, too.

"Gents, he's got to find us before we find the big herd being driven west. He's got to do whatever he can to provide those rustlers time to widen the distance. As far as we know, we're the only riders likely to try and find the cattle. He knows that."

Hernan' smiled. "So if we can, we find him first and put him afoot."

Chet had a question. "How do we find him, Mr. Castleton?"

"We turn back and ride toward Hermasillo. He'll be coming from that direction." Ken arose and flexed his legs. Sitting on the ground had, the last few years, made rising more uncomfortable than it had been a few years earlier.

They brought in the horses, got ready to ride, and left the little dead supper fire, heading southeasterly.

Ken's worry was that if Sheriff Brown knew the course the FM cattle were being driven, he might take a different route, but that was something he tried to compensate for by stringing his companions out so that, whether or not they actually saw Walt Brown and his possemen, they would at least hear them. The possibility of a band of riders being abroad in the small hours of a chilly night for legitimate reasons was slight, especially on Miller ranch land.

Brown himself would not be out there, either, if he didn't think his escaped prisoners might reach the cattle before he could, and that would create more problems than Brown could resolve.

The reason for his anxiety would be something Castleton and the vaqueros would discover if they found the herd. It was something Sheriff Brown had to prevent at all costs.

The night was turning downright cold. The sky was beginning to seem slightly overcast. Occasionally the moon was hidden. Starshine remained bright in the places where the thickening overcast did not interfere with their glow.

The land was empty for miles, except for one interlude when the advancing strung-out horsemen started up a band of coyotes who were gorging on an old carcass of some kind. They were very hungry, otherwise they would have detected the oncoming horsemen. By the time they looked up and saw ghostly horsemen approaching, they made a high squeaking shrill of sound and fled in all directions, small gray wisps racing wildly from what they perceived as a threat to their lives, and it might have been under different circumstances.

Chet rode over a hole in the ground, and after he'd passed, a little owl came out and flew westward on silent wings.

Hernan' came close to Ken. "José was once a horse thief in Mexico," he said. "He even stole horses from the Indians."

Ken nodded about that. To steal horses from some of the most accomplished horse thieves who ever lived, a man had to be exceptionally talented.

They were riding toward a sky that seemed at times to be brightening. It was difficult to be sure because of that overcast, but Ken worried that they might still be riding toward Hermasillo when the light improved, which was something they had to avoid even if it meant abandoning their hunt for Sheriff Brown and his possemen.

A horse whinnied to Castleton's right. He swore under his breath. Chet was down there. Hernan' rode away without a word and Gregorio came out of the gloom to say, "There are horses ahead and south of us." He shrugged. "It could be loose stock."

But it wasn't loose stock. Hernan' loped up to say, "Riders," and pointed southeasterly. As he dropped his arm he also said, "Chet is coming back. I'll find José. Gregorio, you stay here."

Before Ken could speak Hernan' had whirled away. "Send José," he said, speaking so softly Ken could hardly hear. "He knows how to do these things. He can find them without anyone knowing."

Ken nodded. He and Gregorio remained stationary until Chet arrived. As though anticipating disapproval, Chet said, "It wasn't my horse, Mr. Castleton."

Ken wished it had been. If it was one of the posse riders' mounts that had caught the scent of other horses in the night, his whinny would have alerted Sheriff Brown and his riders. If the fugitives were discovered before they found the other horsemen, it would amount to a disaster.

He asked what Chet had heard. The youth answered in few words. "Riders. Maybe quite a bunch. Comin' in south of us from the stage road."

It had to be the sheriff. Ken waited until Hernan' and José returned, then sent Hernan' to find the possemen and to keep them in sight. As the *mayordomo* rode away Gregorio wagged his head. There was definitely a sliver of bluish gray light in the east. Whatever they did had to be done soon, otherwise the sheriff would see them. It was mostly open grassland they'd traversed since leaving the foothills. Getting caught out there would be bad even if they weren't outnumbered.

Ken finally rode at a dead walk southward, taking two of Anna Marie's vaqueros with him. Not a word was spoken. Walking horses made very little noise, so they rode at that gait until Hernan' appeared out of the gloom with his right arm up and rigid. Now, finally, they all heard the riders from Hermasillo.

José said, "It would have been better if we could have caught them in camp."

It was doubtful if the possemen had camped, not if they'd ridden from town only a few hours before.

Ken swung off to stand listening. It was impossible to discern the numbers without getting close enough to see them — and probably be seen in turn. But it sounded like at least four riders and it could have been six or seven.

Abruptly the invisible riders halted. The men with Ken listened intently while standing at the muzzles of their animals to prevent nickering.

Moments later they struck out again. They were riding in a northwesterly direction. In that direction lay the foothills and, almost certainly, the herd of stolen cattle a goodly distance farther along.

When the possemen resumed their ride José grumbled under his breath. "Someone took on too much coffee back in Hermasillo." The others remained silent, willing to accept José's guess.

José also said, "There is a patch of mesquite on their route. Hernan', you know the spot.

It's where that old horned cow chased you. Remember?"

The *mayordomo* remembered and raised his rein hand, but José wasn't finished. "Wait," he told Hernan'. "They could hear us, too. We have to scatter a little, make it sound like loose horses."

They rode slowly for a hundred yards, until José made a gesture, then they moved out a little before loping. Once, when they halted to listen, the night behind them was silent. The possemen had heard them. Whatever they did next would depend upon whether the deception worked.

By the time they reached the flourishing thicket of mesquite José had aimed for, they were a fair distance from each other and riding at different gaits.

Ken thought the ruse would have fooled him, especially since Sheriff Brown, and perhaps several of his companions, knew there would be loose horses on the upper FM range.

They wasted no time waiting to see whether the possemen would resume their course, or whether they might change it, which would have been the prudent thing to do, but Sheriff Brown's concentration was on reaching the foothill country as swiftly as possible. Everything he had and everything he needed was tied in to reaching the stolen herd as swiftly as possible, and in convincing the drovers up there that any riders they might see down their back trail were outlaws after the cattle.

Walt Brown shrugged off the sound of scattered horses, even when the town blacksmith hinted that he did not like this. They were after four fugitives, and although the sounds had seemed to be made by more than four horses, he objected to the fact that those horses they had heard, loose stock or not, had cut across in front of them several hundred yards ahead.

The sheriff's reply to that was an irritated growl. "If it's them — that's why we come out here. But most likely it ain't. They wouldn't be this close to town."

The blacksmith dropped back to ride in silence with the other possemen.

Only after the horses had been tied deep in the thicket and each vaquero had begun slipping through wiry underbrush did they hear the possemen coming ahead again.

José tugged Ken's sleeve and grinned from ear to ear. He was thoroughly enjoying himself whether the others were or not.

Eventually, with that paling predawn sky brightening behind the sheriff and his companions it was possible to count them. Five including Sheriff Brown. Those odds were less formidable. With the advantage of surprise, the odds might even favor the ambushers.

Saying only, "Don't shoot me by mistake," José turned away and worked his way through the thorny brush, getting scratched as he made his way a couple of yards ahead and toward the outer limit of the brush patch. The others watched when he emerged in plain sight, walked a few feet ahead, and dropped to the ground, face down.

No one moved or drew a deep breath as the possemen rode past their hiding place, saw a man sprawled up ahead, and reined to a stop.

Will Clavenger, the blacksmith, let his breath out in an audible hiss and faced toward the brush patch. Everyone else was sitting perfectly still staring at the sprawled man up ahead.

Walt Brown eased up in his saddle to dismount. Several possemen started to follow his example. What stopped them cold was the sound of guns being cocked along the foremost stand of the thicket.

The blacksmith was the first to speak. "Son of a bitch," he exclaimed, and scowled fiercely in the direction of the sheriff. He might not have been the first posseman to realize they had ridden into an ambush, but he was the only vocal one.

Ken hardly raised his voice from concealment in the thicket. "Drop your guns. I said, *drop your guns!*"

One of the possemen groaned loudly as he tossed down his Colt and leaned to draw the carbine butt-first and let it drop.

Sheriff Brown sat up ahead of the others like a statue on horseback, making no move to obey as the men behind him shed their weapons. He had recognized Castleton's voice.

It wasn't Ken who walked slowly up beside the sheriff's horse, grinning from ear to ear as he pointed his gun at Walt Brown, and cocked it. It was José, and there was no mistaking his expression.

Sheriff Brown flung his six-gun away and was leaning over to jettison his booted Winchester when José's gun arm rose in a blur, came down hard, and the sheriff slid from his horse with blood beginning to seep from beneath his hat.

Ken came out of the brush behind the horsemen and ordered them to dismount. Will Clavenger flashed a defiant look downward and said, "This ain't over by a damned sight, cow thief," then came down off his saddle with obvious reluctance.

The men remaining out of sight pushed through and stood with cocked six-guns. A posseman muttered what was probably in the minds of all the men who had been recruited in the middle of the night to ride with Sheriff Brown.

"I knew it, I felt it in my bones." He looked dispassionately at the unconscious man lying in front of José Elizondo. "You damned fool, Sheriff. We tried to tell you to be real careful, but no, you had somethin' else in mind, an' look what happened."

CHAPTER 10

A Cocked Gun

José and Gregorio gathered up all the weapons as Ken told the townsmen to sit down. Hernan' went among their animals picking up reins. He led them out a long distance, turned them loose, and ran them off in several different directions.

The blacksmith glared at Ken. "You're in it up to your neck," he growled. "If you'd had a lick of sense you'd be fifty miles from here by now an' still riding."

Ken eyed Clavenger and answered without raising his voice. "Mister, most likely it didn't dawn on you when you fellers rode down to that abandoned ranch where the FM cattle were, to wonder how your sheriff knew that's where we'd be, and the cattle."

Clavenger was a dogged man, not shrewd like some, but not stupid either.

"Were you with him at the Miller place?" Ken asked him, but the bitter-eyed man refused to answer. Then Ken said, "Didn't you

135

wonder why the sheriff was so dead set on finding us?"

"Sure," snarled the blacksmith. "You busted out of his jailhouse an' that never happened to him before. You was fugitives from the law. What'd you expect him to do, set on his hands in town?"

"I don't think that's why he rousted you fellers out of bed in the middle of the night to go hunting us. Sure, he wanted to know where we were, but after he didn't find us at the ranch he knew what we were up to. He didn't want us to find the herd of FM cattle someone rustled while he was using us, and you, to provide time for the rustlers of the main herd to get far enough away."

Will Clavenger reached into a pocket for a plug of twist without taking his eyes off Ken Castleton. After biting off a sliver and cheeking it, he said, "Walt said you was as slippery as an eel."

Hernan' came up to say the posse horses had been run off. Clavenger gazed at the *mayordomo*. "Hernando," he said in a quiet tone, "how could you let this saddle tramp talk you into this damned trouble?"

Hernan' gazed at the large man from an expressionless face as he spoke. "We didn't rustle those FM cattle. Three strangers did. We were going after them. You know the rest.

136

You fellers from town arrived, believed the lie the sheriff told you, and didn't even go looking around for other tracks of three riders leaving the old ranch."

"What other tracks?" the blacksmith asked scornfully.

José and Gregorio arrived dragging the unconscious lawman. José was grinning as he let Brown's legs drop. He shook his head at the town blacksmith, whom he knew fairly well.

"You'd have found them if you'd looked, but no, you went on what the sheriff told you. And about us ambushing you fellers tonight — why would we bother doin' that except to keep you'n the others from comin' up behind us when we were trying to get back the FM cattle?"

Clavenger looked from Hernan' to Ken Castleton. "What cattle? Sheriff Brown told us you'd be up along the foothills somewhere, an' that was reasonable; you'd need to rest your horses and —"

"We were up near the foothills, blacksmith, because we wanted to find the other stolen cattle."

"What other stolen cattle?"

Hernan' rolled his eyes in exasperation. "The first band was taken down to that old ranch so's you fellers would come down there and grab us, while someone was running off

137

Miz Miller's remaining herd. Four, five hundred head."

Clavenger turned back toward Ken. "What's he talkin' about?"

"Exactly what he said. While you were down yonder catching us, the sheriff's friends were up here stealing the rest of the Miller cattle."

"I don't believe it."

Ken shrugged, gazed at the seated possemen who had been listening, and finally said, "Tell you what, blacksmith. You ride with us until we find the cattle, then you can ask whoever's driving them how they got them."

One of the possemen, a glum-faced man with little hair and a round, chubby face, spoke quietly. "It'd be better than settin' out here in the damned cold, Will."

Clavenger growled a reply to that suggestion as the sheriff began showing signs of life. He groaned, fumbled for a grip on the ground, and pushed himself up into a sitting position. He put both hands to his head. "Anybody got some whiskey?" he moaned.

No one had and now the possemen were regarding him from expressionless faces. José walked over, sank to one knee in front of the lawman, and smiled from ear to ear as he lifted out his six-gun and cocked it. Sheriff Brown's head came up.

José said, "I could have killed you. I think I will do it now," and lowered his gun barrel until it was aimed at Walt Brown's soft parts.

The sheriff forgot his oversized headache, his eyes widened. He risked a look at the watching men and bleated, "Do something. He's crazy, look at him. *Do something!*"

Until Ken spoke no one said a word, partly because they were convinced that if anyone moved José would squeeze the trigger, partly because they'd had time to weigh what Ken had told Will Clavenger, and whether they believed it or not, some of it was very probable.

"Leave it be, José."

José continued to grin at Sheriff Brown. "He deserves it, Ken. He stole cattle from the Miller outfit. If Mr. Miller was alive he'd shoot him an' I wouldn't have to."

The blacksmith had watched Walt Brown's face throughout this dangerous period and finally said, "Sheriff, they told us you was involved in runnin' off several hundred head of Miller cattle. They told us they were trying to find them when we came along . . . Sheriff?"

José stopped smiling, and tipped his gun barrel a little until it pointed at the sheriff's breastbone. He said, "Pray, *amigo*. Ten seconds to pray."

139

Hernan' and Gregorio had guns in their hands, waiting. Ken Castleton was motionless. If there was going to be an execution he could not reach José before the vaquero pulled the trigger.

Sheriff Brown had sweat on his face in the cold morning light. "All right," he said in a husky voice. "All right. We sold Miller cattle to a free grazer. He didn't say where he was goin' with them, except it'd be west to a gunsight pass out of Thunder Valley and beyond."

Clavenger looked stunned. The other possemen reacted in different ways. José eased down the dog of his six-gun and when Sheriff Brown saw him do this, he blew out a ragged breath, convinced he had just been as close to death as he would ever be until his final passing.

Ken asked the name of the free grazer.

Sheriff Brown seemed to have come down from his mortal fear. He said, "I don't remember his name."

José cocked the six-gun again, and smiled.

"His name's Headly, Matt Headly. I ran across him some time back. He was lookin' for cattle to buy. . . . John Lytle knew him from somewhere. John, Pete Fincher, and the 'breed called Tom hired on with Headly to

140

round up the cattle and drive them out of the country."

A posseman asked if Headly had paid Sheriff Brown for the cattle. The sheriff's eyes went to that bent finger inside the trigger guard before he replied. "Yes. He paid me in town a while back."

"He knew they would be stolen cattle?"

Brown shrugged. "I never told him that, only that I knew where there was a lot of cattle up near the foothills that he could drive off real easy, and that I'd see to it that he got a long head start before anyone missed the cattle."

Hernan' looked dourly at the lawman. "So you had them steal a hundred head and drive them down to that old ranch to give Headly time."

"Yes."

Hernan' turned and gave the blacksmith a pained look. Clavenger ignored Hernan'. He was staring at Sheriff Brown. "You son of a bitch," he said. "Vaquero, go ahead and pull the trigger."

The men held their breath. José tipped his gun barrel up and down several times, then, still grinning from ear to ear, eased down the hammer and arose as he leathered his weapon. As far as he was concerned, he had just been repaid for his humiliation at the hands of Walt Brown.

The blacksmith cheeked a chew and gazed at the other possemen. "Well? . . ."

That round-faced man with thinning hair shoved up to his feet, spat aside, and regarded the sheriff as he spoke. "Walt, I won't say I'm surprised, but you sure hung yourself this time." He shifted his attention to Ken. "I'll ride with you, if you'd like. You got any idea where the Miller cattle are by now?"

Ken had none because he did not know the country that well, but Hernan' did. "The gunsight pass he talked of is about twelve miles from where we are right now. By now the free grazer ought to be close to it or maybe on through to the open country on the far side. At the least we got maybe a fifteen-mile ride." Hernan' pointed at the sheriff. "What do we do with him?"

Ken said, "José, you an' Gregorio see if you can find their horses. You saw 'em last, Hernan', you go with them. When you get back we'll take Sheriff Brown with us. He'll know the free grazer."

As the vaqueros departed Clavenger went to the carelessly cast aside weapons, selected his six-gun and his Winchester, and looked balefully at Ken. "Everybody makes mistakes. I ain't apologizin' but I'll ride with you."

Ken asked a lean, short, wiry-looking posseman if he would ride to the Miller place

142

and explain things to Anna Marie Miller. The man was agreeable.

But it was a long two hours before the vaqueros had found all the loose saddle stock and hazed it back. By then there was heat in the new day, so before saddling the horses were watered then led back to be rigged out.

As they were mounting Ken asked if the blacksmith would take the reins of the sheriff's horse and Clavenger agreed with a short nod of the head.

They had a long ride ahead of them so they spared their horses rather than try to hasten. The heat was less because of an accumulation of galleon-sized big white clouds moving majestically, but very slowly, down across Thunder Valley.

Hernan' and one posseman rode up ahead with Ken. Hernan' knew the land and used every available shortcut to minimize the riding they had to do. But that only helped a little.

The sun reached its zenith and was coasting down the westerly sky when Hernan' returned from a scout up ahead to say that he had located the trail of the drive, so they veered in that direction. By midafternoon they saw the gunsight pass through the high hills that encircled Thunder Valley.

It was a considerable distance ahead and because there was no dust, they assumed the free grazer had got through and out of the valley.

One posseman rode beside Sheriff Brown, whose demeanor was sour and had been since they'd started the ride. The possemen evidently knew Walt Brown well because he addressed him by his first name, not as sheriff the way most of the other men addressed him.

The posseman said, "Walt, why Miller cattle? There are other, bigger herds around."

Sheriff Brown ignored the question, but a mile or so farther along he looked at the posseman and said, "Jim, when Fred was alive things was different. Since *she's* been in charge she'd hardly give me the time of day."

Will Clavenger, on the sheriff's opposite side, made a growly comment. "I don't blame her, the way you used to ride out there and spend the day. You made it obvious you'd like to take Fred's place, and hell, Walt, knowing as much about you as I do now, you couldn't stand in Fred's shadow."

Hernan' rode ahead again as they neared the pass out of Thunder Valley. The others watched him in thoughtful silence. When he returned a half hour later he said, "They're through the pass."

Gregorio had a question. "Did you go to the top to see where they are on the other side?"

Hernan' hadn't. He hadn't wanted to take

144

the time but when they could clearly see sign that a fair-sized herd of cattle had gone up through there, he loped ahead again.

This time when he returned there were long shadows and a noticeable coolness to the dying day. The entire cavalcade halted at a creek to water the livestock, and Hernan' told them the drive was raising dust on a southward angle, which made sense; no one who free grazed his way through the country would turn north at this time of year. If he did he'd end up over the line in Colorado where leaves were already turning and the grass had headed out and was about as nutritious as cotton, and as tasteless.

When they headed up into the pass the smell of cattle was still strong. It was also darker in there than it had been behind them where nothing interfered with the weakening daylight.

Until now Sheriff Brown had said very little. When he did speak he revealed a better knowledge of Thunder Valley and its environs than someone from town would be expected to know. He said there was a wider, level place up near the top of the pass where there was feed for the animals and flat ground for bedrolls.

Ken and Hernan' exchanged a look. Walt Brown had already proved he was sly and clever. He had just now said something that indicated he had probably gone over the same ground the free grazer had taken. Ken wondered to himself just how long the sheriff had been planning his raid, but he slouched along in silence until one of the possemen said he thought his horse was laming up.

They halted to dismount and inspect the animal. Will Clavenger lifted the sore front hoof, cleaned it with his pocketknife, probed until he found the sore spot, and carved above the shoe until he dislodged a pebble half as wide as a man's thumb.

Without a word he went forward, swung back into the saddle, and led off with the reins of Sheriff Brown's horse looped loosely around his saddle horn.

They arrived at the broad summit where grass grew and several squatty oaks made shadows, swung off, and when Ken and Hernan' walked ahead to the downslope, several possemen trudged after them.

The view was spectacular, even in poor light they could see for miles. They were up there when dusk began to settle and Ken raised his arm to point.

"Light," he said. "Someone out there has fired up some twigs for a supper fire."

There were two cooking fires but one was more difficult to see because of trees. A posseman asked how far and Hernan' replied, "Six, eight miles."

"Hell," the posseman exclaimed. "They should have been farther along than that, shouldn't they?"

No one answered. Ken and Hernan' exchanged a wink about townsmen's ignorance about how slowly cattle had to be driven.

CHAPTER 11

Settling Old Scores

They debated about sneaking up on the drovers in the dark. Will Clavenger was especially keen on the idea, but the vaqueros were not. The horses needed rest and time to browse. As Gregorio said, if they got down out of the pass before daylight they could cover the distance because by then their animals would be fit again.

But it was Hernan' who put forth the best argument. "There are nine of us. We don't have to sneak up on them and maybe get shot in the night."

"Ten," a posseman muttered and Hernan' gave the speaker a withering look. "Nine. Sheriff Brown don't count," and resumed his comment.

"If it's only the free grazer and those bastards who led us down to the old abandoned ranch, we'll outnumber them three to one." He smiled. "Let them see us coming. Let them see us and begin to sweat. Maybe by then they'll know they can't make a fight of it."

Ken asked the sheriff if the free grazer had riders of his own and got a bitter wag of the head for his answer.

That settled it, the men unwound their blankets and bedded down. Sometime in the night the cold increased very noticeably.

In the morning when they arose, shivering and silent, to bring in the animals for saddling, they were mindful of a horse's objection to cold blankets on their backs, and even more mindful of steel bits as cold as ice. José swung up and his horse immediately lowered its head and bucked. As the others watched, José freed his shot-loaded rawhide quirt, an indispensable part of every vaquero's outfit, and swung it by the loop so that it stung the horse's belly when it came down. The horse ceased its antics. José swore at him as the others turned their horses several times before mounting and got astride without trouble.

Hernan' and Gregorio exchanged a look; no one in his right mind did what José had done. He should have known better, and he undoubtedly did, but being careless had shaken the last cobwebs from his mind.

The blacksmith jerked his head curtly for Sheriff Brown to get astride, then looped the reins to Brown's horse as he'd done before, and followed Ken Castleton's lead as the riders started the descent on the far side of the pass.

It was dark and cold. The men suffered a little but their mounts didn't, they moved out willingly.

The descent was more precipitous than the ascent had been. Horses had a knack for sensing terrain in darkness or in daylight. They avoided slippery places and sidestepped rocks.

By the time they were out of Thunder Valley on level ground the animals had been warmed up. Their riders, too, were beginning to have less stiffness although the chill remained.

Ken led off in a lope for a little more than a mile, by which time the sky was beginning to pale a little.

They alternately loped and walked until they could hear cattle bawling.

Ahead in the near distance the bawling seemed to be louder as their drovers tried to line up their drive after picking up strays and laggards, forcing them to bunch up with the rest of the cattle.

Ken halted, then held up his hand and pointed. Several hundred head of cattle were slightly south of them, moving stiffly and still protesting.

The men driving them were not visible until the sky brightened a little more. Hernan' stood in his stirrups, satisfied they would now recover the FM cattle, and concerned about the number of drovers.

Sheriff Brown, back beside Will Clavenger, said, "Four. I told you he hired three and he didn't have no other riders."

No one heeded the sheriff except the blacksmith. He spoke in a low growl to the man whose horse he was leading. "You better be right, Sheriff, because if you ain't an' there's trouble, you'll be the first casualty."

Sheriff Brown and Clavenger exchanged a long stare of mutual animosity, after which the sheriff said no more.

They rode a short distance, until they could verify that there were only four riders working at keeping the herd moving, and too busy at their work to look back.

The next time they dropped back to a walk they were close enough to see the drovers clearly, and at about that time someone up ahead looked back.

The pursuing horseman clearly heard that drover's warning yell. By that time the possemen, the vaqueros, and Ken Castleton were within carbine range.

The free grazer and his riders came together behind the herd.

Hernan' came ahead to ride stirrup with Ken. He had the tie-down thong holding his Colt in its holster hanging loose as he said,

151

"That one in the middle is Pete Fincher."

The cattle, no longer being hurried along, were fanning out to find grass. They were no longer complaining.

Ken continued to walk his horse. Its leggy stride carried him slightly ahead of the men farther back. Hernan' had to keep his mount reaching out to stay abreast.

Up ahead a man whose old slouch hat hid some of his face, and who hadn't been near a barber in months, sat with both gloved hands atop the saddle horn masticating on his first chew of the day. His stubbly face showed only the gentle movements of his jaw, and there was the steel butt plate of a booted Winchester jutting upward on the right side.

Ken recognized the other three. From his first meeting of them when they'd come to his camp to try and take Betsy Conners away, he remembered each hard face and each horse they were astride.

When both parties were no more than a hundred yards or so apart, the stubbly-faced, raffish-looking man with the slouched hat raised his arm high, palm forward, the age-old sign of welcome.

Hernan' glanced at the man beside him. Ken did not return the greeting, but kept on riding until the distance had been whittled down to no more than a hundred or so feet, then he drew rein and leaned on his saddle horn gazing from one drover to the others.

Behind him, the possemen spread out slightly and the vaqueros, never noted for caution, rode steadily ahead three abreast and halted just behind Ken and Hernan'.

The raffish man smiled and said, "Good morning, gents."

Ken studied the man before speaking. The free grazer was typical of his kind. He was falsely affable in the face of difficulties, looked weathered and faded, and as sly as a fox with sharp features and sunken eyes that were barely discernible the way he wore his old hat pulled well forward.

Ken leaned on his saddle horn. "Mister, you're in bad company," he replied. "Good morning to you. . . . Now then, each one of you turn your horses with the left side facing us, and get down."

The free grazer's smile broadened. "Well now, gents," he said, "ain't no call to be hard-nosed."

"Turn the horses and get down!"

The free grazer set the example by dismounting so that the possemen and their companions could watch everything he did. He was still wearing the unctuous, fixed smile when he told his riders to get down, too.

They did, and stood with their backs to their

horses. By now they had all recognized Sheriff Brown, and had also noticed that his horse was being led by its reins. They could put only one interpretation on that.

"Now the guns," Ken told them. "Be real careful, gents. Out here in the open you don't have the chance of a snowball in hell. *Get rid of the guns!*"

This time it required a little more time for the order to be obeyed, and the last man to shuck his sidearm was Pete Fincher, the cold-eyed man with thin lips.

Ken said, "Hernan,' you lads take care of those other three. Free grazer, you got a name?"

As the vaqueros rode closer before dismounting in front of the drover's hired men, the free grazer spread his hands, palms down as he replied to Ken's question. "Name's Matt Headly. What's your name, mister?"

Ken ignored the question. "Mr. Headly, you recognize the feller on the led horse?"

The other man's little eyes went to Sheriff Brown and narrowed slightly as Matt Headly's thoughts scrambled in an effort to come up with a noncommittal reply. "Well now, friend, I do believe I've seen him somewhere before, but a man meets lots of folks in my line of work."

The mustanger's eyes showed cold humor.

"In your line of work, I'd bet you've run across a few lawmen. Tell me something, Mr. Headly, do you have a bill of sale for those cattle you've been driving?"

This time the free grazer's answer was short. "Sure have," he said, and fished among his pockets until he came up with a limp and rumpled scrap of paper. He held it out.

Ken took it, flattened it, and read. He reread it, folded it, and put it in his pocket looking coldly at the free grazer. "You know who signed it, Mr. Headly?"

"Yes sir. It's right there on the bottom of the paper. Someone named Miz Anna Marie Miller."

"And who gave it you, Mr. Headly?"

"That gent with the star on his shirt."

"But you weren't sure you'd ever seen him before."

"No sir, that's not what I said. I told you I believed I'd maybe seen him somewhere before."

Will Clavenger growled a curse at the free grazer. "You're one breath away from getting shot for cattle stealing, you son of a bitch. One more damned lie out of you an' I'll personally wring your neck."

Matt Headly stared at the massive, bearded blacksmith, and did not cringe, but made a candid statement. "Mister, I didn't steal no

155

cattle. Your friend here's got my bill of sale."

Clavenger glared in bleak silence as Matt Headly faced Ken Castleton again. "Mister, you saw the bill of sale, properly signed an' all. If you boys come onto me to make trouble I'll take you to court sure as you're standing there."

Ken shifted weight from one leg to the other when he replied. "That depends on whether you'll be able to take anyone to court or not." He looked around, the nearest stand of trees were about a half mile northward. Headly might have been puzzled by the way Castleton looked over the countryside, but he had no trouble at all understanding it when Castleton stepped back to his horse and began freeing his lasso rope.

He said, "Wait a minute, mister. Just a damned minute. You prove to me that-there bill of sale ain't valid an' get my money back for me, an' you can have the damned cattle."

Ken continued freeing his rope and turned almost casually as he said, "Get your money back from who?"

"From him. The sheriff. I paid him cash on the barrelhead for them cattle an' he give me that bill of sale."

Every eye turned to Walt Brown. He sat his saddle gazing balefully at Matt Headly, until Ken spoke again.

"Mr. Headly, the bill of sale isn't worth a damn. Anna Marie Miller didn't sign it."

The sheriff interrupted. "How d'you know she didn't? She signed it an' in the eyes of the law that bill of sale's a legal document."

Ken leaned across the seat of his saddle looking at Sheriff Brown. He did not say anything for a while, then all he said was, "Let's go back and see."

Headly squawked. "Back where? Mister, I got a big herd of cattle to get down to good feed."

"Back to the Miller ranch, Mr. Headly, and show your paper to Miz Miller. If she says she signed it, then I'll apologize an' you can be on your way."

"Them damned cattle'll drift to hell an' gone."

Ken smiled. "We'll come back and help you round them up. They won't go far, it's not that long a ride to the Miller place."

Matt Headly glared from beneath his pulled-down hat brim. He gave an excellent imitation of an outraged individual, so good that several of the possemen began to have doubts, and well they might. Headly did have a bill of sale. The possemen had not seen the signature.

Ken faced back around with the lasso rope in his hand. "It's your choice," he told the free grazer, and moved to shake out a small loop.

Headly spat, glared from Sheriff Brown to Ken, looked over where his hired riders were being watched by three capable-looking vaqueros, and made a great flourish of throwing up his arms in resignation.

"All right, but Mr. Whatever-your-name-is, if this turns out bad, I'm comin' after your hide!"

Ken ignored the threat to ask a question. "You said you paid cash on the barrelhead?"

"That's exactly what I done. An' it cleaned me out to do it, but the price was right."

Ken nodded. "I'll bet it was." He gestured. "Get on your horse." As this order was being obeyed Ken nodded in Hernan' Iturbide's direction. "Tie their hands behind their backs and lead their horses."

There was a small delay. Gregorio, going through a saddlebag behind one of the men being tied astride, came across three cans of peaches and some cans of sardines.

It had been a long time since Castleton and the FM riders had eaten. As they held back to take the edge off their hunger, that round-faced posseman from Hermasillo, the man with the thin hair, went ahead to plunder the saddlebags of the other two hired riders and the raffish man who had hired them.

158

There was enough food for all the men riding with Castleton to take the pleats out of their stomachs. They did not offer a morsel to Headly or the men sitting astride with arms lashed in back.

The sun was nearing its meridian before the cavalcade got under way, and from the top of the pass when they looked back, the cattle were indeed beginning to spread out. Matt Headly groaned about this and shook his head, but said nothing until Gregorio eased up beside him and, leaning from the saddle with his wandering eye making a slow circle as his good eye became fixed on Headly, asked in almost a whisper how much money he had, and Matt Headly shook his head. "No more'n a few dollars. Payin' for them damned cattle just about cleaned me out."

"And," asked the man with the disconcerting eye, "what did you plan to pay those three hired riders with? *Amigo,* you have a money belt under your shirt. I saw the bulge when we first met. Reach in there, unbuckle it, and give it to me. Don't raise your voice."

Half the other men saw Gregorio and guessed what he was about, the other half didn't, but if they had seen the free grazer pull out his money belt and hand it to the vaquero, they wouldn't have said a word.

Ken and Hernan' were riding ahead as

Gregorio, with the money belt slung over one shoulder, dropped back to ride with José and Chet.

Not until they were back in Thunder Valley with the sun beginning its long downward slide, did Sheriff Brown call to Ken Castleton that the Mexican with the cockeye had robbed Matt Headly.

Ken twisted in the saddle, saw the sheriff and farther back Gregorio and José riding together, and said, "He didn't take anywhere nearly as much as you took from the free grazer," and sat forward as Hernan' began building one of his black-paper cigarillos.

Gregorio looked around for Chet, rolled both his eyes, and smiled. The youngest rider among them smiled back. He had been eating an apple raided from someone's saddlebag, and flung away the core as Hernan' stood in his stirrups and said, "Riders." Before Ken could speak, Hernan' giggled his mount over into a lope as though to scout up the distant strangers.

There was no reason to halt and await the *mayordomo*'s return; what appeared as little more than ant-sized movement far ahead on a slightly northwesterly course, did not appear to be more than a couple of riders, perhaps at the most three of them.

Will Clavenger asked Sheriff Brown where

the money was that Matt Headly had paid him, and instead of an answer got a mean look and a sneer.

Clavenger leaned down slowly and straightened back with a wicked bladed boot knife in his hand. He did not say a word, but he reeled in the reins to the sheriff's horse until the lawman was close, and pushed out the knife until it touched Walt Brown's shirt. For a couple of yards they rode like that, before a posseman up ahead saw them and said, "Push, Will. Lean on it a little."

Other riders looked. None of them said a word. The blacksmith did lean, just enough to draw blood through the sheriff's shirt.

Walt Brown's voice was a mixture of fear and repressed fury when he said, "It's hid in town. What the hell's got into you, Will?"

The gleaming blade did not move back. "I never told you, did I, that the two most worthless folks on the face of the earth, in my opinion, is liars and thieves. I'd as soon cut you open as look at you."

"Damn it, we've known each other ten, twelve years," exclaimed the sheriff, and with everyone but the two men up ahead watching, Clavenger leaned again, drew more blood, then sat back in his saddle and sheathed the boot knife. "When we get back to town, you're goin' to lead me to your cache. Sheriff,

161

you hoodwinked me. I never liked havin' anyone make a fool out of me. . . . If the law
don't hang you or send you to prison for a
long time, I'm goin' to hunt you down no
matter where you go, an' cut your damned
throat!"

Hernan' trotted back to say that he could
state only that there were two, not three, riders on the same course the possemen and their
companions were pursuing. When a posseman
growled about Hernan' not getting closer than
he had, the *mayordomo* twisted with one hand
on his mount's rump and replied, "You go
charge at them, an' we'll maybe have to bury
you."

Little more was said until the oncoming pair
of riders were close enough for Hernan' to
gasp before speaking again. "*Santa Maria*
. . . I know that stocking-footed chestnut
horse." José and Gregorio said almost the same
thing at the same time.

Ken looked questioningly at the *mayordomo*.
Hernan' said, "*Señora* Miller."

Ken tipped down his hat, which helped
slightly, but he still was not sure it was the
man he'd sent to the ranch to tell Anna Marie
what was happening, until both sets of riders
got closer, then he recognized the man and
the woman.

He shook his head. If he'd known she was

going to get the man to guide her back up here he would not have sent him. He looked like hell, was unshaven, unwashed, his clothing was soiled and rumpled, and at this time he would have preferred meeting anyone including scalp hunters, rather than Anna Marie Miller.

He did not feel up to fencing with her, either. He was tired all the way through.

CHAPTER 12

Tired Men

Anna Marie had plenty of time to study the oncoming riders. What she wanted most to hear was that they had been successful in locating her stolen cattle.

She halted near a spindly tree and sat in its shade waiting. Ken Castleton, like those around him, said nothing as they came up to the tree and drew rein.

Anna Marie looked for Chet, let her gaze slide next to Sheriff Brown, from there to her vaqueros, and lastly to Ken Castleton. She said, "Who is he?" and jutted her jaw in the direction of the free grazer.

Before the others could reply Matt Headly started complaining. "Lady, I'm bein' dragooned. Mostly by that stocky feller the others call Ken. Lady, I got a bill of sale to them cattle I been driving. I ain't done no wrong to nobody."

Anna Marie waited until Headly had finished, then leaned over to dismount. The posseman swung off beside her. She nodded at the free grazer. "I'd like to see your bill of sale."

Before the free grazer could reply Ken Castleton dismounted a trifle stiffly, produced a stub of a pencil, the bill of sale which he turned face down against his saddle, and asked Anna Marie to sign her name.

She responded slowly, but did eventually walk over and with the scent of violets reaching Castleton, she took the pencil without looking at him and signed her name.

Castleton turned the bill of sale over, looked briefly at the signature on the bottom of the piece of paper, then walked over to Matt Headly and held up the paper, turning it from one side to the other.

Headly squirmed as Ken passed the paper to Will Clavenger, whose formidable scowl deepened as he silently handed the paper back. "Ain't no comparison at all," he exclaimed.

The last person Ken showed the bill of sale to, first one side, then the other side, was Sheriff Brown. The lawman's jaw muscles rippled and he glared from the paper to Ken without saying a word.

Ken held the paper up for the others to see, waited a long moment, then reversed it. There was a murmur among the riders. Chet said, "Blacksmith's right. They don't even look alike." His gaze lifted to Sheriff Brown as Anna Marie approached Castleton, took the paper from him, and examined it for some time. When she had finished she handed back the paper, said nothing, and returned to her horse. From the saddle she gazed bitterly upon Walt Brown.

"My husband's friend. How could you do such a thing, Sheriff?"

Matt Headly wanted his paper back. Ken smiled as he put it back into his pocket and went over to his horse before speaking again.

One of the men who had said almost nothing all morning finally spoke. It was the lipless man with the bold eyes and the long nose. "Lady, Mr. Headly told us he had the bill of sale. We hired on to help him drive the cattle. That's all."

Hernan' reddened in anger. "You lie! You and those men beside you drove the first band of stolen FM cattle south to that old ranch. You did that to draw the Miller ranch riders after the cattle. The sheriff had already sent riders down there to catch us. It was you and your friends who left the cattle at the old ranch. You then took your companions and rode hard to get back to the Miller ranch and steal the rest of the cattle. I don't think you're smart enough to have planned all that, but I think *he's* that smart." Hernan' pointed at Sheriff

Brown, dropped his arm, and glared. "When the *patrón* was alive, when we caught men like you, we hanged them on the nearest tree."

Hernan's anger softened a little, his color returned to normal, and he loosened a little, but his hostile stare at Fincher lingered.

Anna Marie returned to her horse, turned before mounting, and said, "Mr. Castleton, what did you have in mind?"

"Taking them to Hermasillo and locking them up."

Anna Marie swung up across leather before speaking again. "Chet, ride back with me. I don't like leaving your sister alone. Mr. Castleton, when you've finished in town I'd like to see you at the ranch."

Chet kneed his mount forward and as Anna Marie turned her back on the tired, unshaven men, Chet rode with her.

Matt Headly watched them and sighed. "That's one fine-lookin' female," he observed, and for that remark got a venomous glare from the three outlaws, Sheriff Brown, and Ken Castleton.

The ride toward town was resumed, with even less said than before the encounter near the shade tree. The horses hung in their bits, the men were no less tired, and as sunshine increased the warmth, they had to fight against dozing off. The blacksmith was not one of

167

them. He eased up beside Castleton and said, "Folks in town ain't goin' to believe the sheriff did all this. He's been a fixture around Hermasillo a long time."

Ken thought Clavenger was probably right and nodded without speaking. Not until the blacksmith said the rest of what was in his mind.

"Mr. Castleton, unless you'n the vaqueros figure to stay in town an' keep folks away from the jailhouse, someone'll bust Walt Brown, an' maybe even those friends of his, out of their cells."

Before they had rooftops in sight, with the sun settling steadily lower toward some sawtooth distant peaks, they halted at a creek to let the horses tank up. Then they rode on.

When the cavalcade rode down Main Street in Hermasillo there were few pedestrians in sight. It was suppertime. But they were seen by enough people for word to spread rapidly.

The possemen led their horses toward the livery barn, excepting the men who owned the horses they had ridden. These riders led their horses home to be fed, perhaps grained a little, and left to fill up on rough hay.

Hernan' and Gregorio offered to take Castleton's horse to the livery barn to be fed and rested. He had them herd the prisoners

168

to a cell, after going over each man for a hide-out weapon, and locked them in.

When the office was finally quiet Ken went to sit at Sheriff Brown's desk, cock up his feet, and toss his hat aside.

He was as tired as he'd ever been before. Not entirely from physical exhaustion, although that certainly was part of it, he was tired from the mental strain and anxiety. Until they had come onto the stolen FM cattle, and had the free grazer as well as Sheriff Brown's three outlaws disarmed, he'd lived with nagging doubts, the kind that wore a man down almost as much as missing food and sleep would do.

Eventually, he left the jailhouse, went over to the café, which was nearly empty, and ordered supper. The café man as well as his few customers stared at Ken. Never having seen him before, it was almost uncanny how they knew who he was.

When the café owner brought his laden platter and coffee, he said, "I saw you'n the fellers from town take Walt Brown an' some other fellers into the jailhouse with their wrists tied."

Ken looked up. His reply was simple. "Did you?"

The man pointed to his front window. Ken smiled and attacked his meal. The café man and the other few patrons of his diner exchanged looks, and the other diners arose one at a time and departed. Castleton paused for a moment to gaze at the man. "Word'll spread now, won't it?"

The café owner decided he did not like Ken's attitude, nodded woodenly, and returned to his cooking area where he slammed pots and pans around in anger.

When the man returned to the counter, Will Clavenger was sitting beside Castleton. The blacksmith barely more than glanced up when he said, "Coffee!"

The café man brought it, refilled Ken's cup, and without a word returned to his cooking area. Ken was irritating enough, but the café man had seen the blacksmith clean out an entire saloon without resorting to weapons. At this point the better part of valor was prudence.

Clavenger said he had eaten at home and leaned toward Ken with both large fists clasped atop the counter as he said, "Talked to a couple fellers on the town council. Told 'em the whole blessed story and told 'em I wanted to fill in for sheriff until other arrangements could be made."

Ken looked around. "And they agreed?"

The blacksmith was staring bleakly at his fists when he replied. "No. They said it'd have

170

to wait until the council met in broad daylight, then there'd be a decision."

Ken continued to gaze at the burly, large man. "Do you want the sheriff's job?" he asked, and received a blunt answer.

"I do. I watched Walt over the years. It's not just this latest mess, I've seen him do other things. He ain't fit for the badge he wears."

"You've got a good business at the forge, haven't you?"

"Yes, but that's not it, Mr. Castleton. A sheriff should obey the law he hands out to others. Ain't nothin' worse than a dishonest lawman."

Ken went back to his meal. He had known before entering the café that he was hungry, but until supper had been placed before him he'd had no idea *how* hungry.

The blacksmith drank his coffee, put a small coin beside the cup, and left. After his departure the café man returned looking troubled. He had heard everything the blacksmith had said.

He sat on a tall stool in front of his pie table and watched Castleton eat for a moment before speaking. "I'm on the town council," he said, and watched Ken mopping up gravy as he nodded his head without looking at the man.

"Will'd be a good man for Walt's job, but

he hasn't went out of his way to be real friendly."

Ken finished with the gravy-soaked bread, fished out his bandanna, and vigorously wiped his fingers. He then pushed the empty platter away and pulled in the coffee cup. Finally, he looked over at the man on the stool. "He'd make a good lawman, mister. I've ridden with him a fair bit lately. He don't take sass and he don't back down."

"But he's rubbed some folks the wrong way over the years. There might be complaints if the council appointed him to Walt Brown's job until the next election."

"When will that be?" Ken asked.

"Couple years."

"What did you say your name was?"

"I didn't say, but it's Hendry — that's with a *d* — Hendry Fisk."

Castleton nodded acceptance of the introduction and leaned back off the bench as though preparing to arise when he said, "Mr. Fisk, let me ask you a question. You folks in Hermasillo want a sheriff who goes around kissing babies or do you want a man who would never try to bankrupt a widow-woman by stealing and selling her cattle?"

Ken did not await the reply, which never came. He tossed silver coins atop the counter, turned, and walked out of the café.

Across the road Hernan', Gregorio, and José were sprawling on the bench in front of the jailhouse. As he approached them, José said, "All right for us to go eat now?"

Ken looked surprised. "You could have eaten any time. Sure, go ahead."

As the three men arose from the bench Gregorio sounded almost plaintive. "But someone had to be over here in case the sheriff's friends came."

Ken snorted. "What friends he's got are sleeping like logs."

When Ken entered the lighted jailhouse office a wiry man was holding a cocked six-gun. It was aimed in the direction of the door. As soon as the former posseman recognized Ken he eased the dog down and offered a lopsided grin accompanied by a small shrug.

"In case a mob come an' got past them Miller ranch vaqueros," he explained.

The posseman remained standing after Castleton sat down. "They've been raising hell down in their cells. They ain't been fed."

Castleton pulled some wrinkled greenbacks from a pocket and held them out. "Get some grub over at the café. Hernan' is over there, he'n the others can bring it back."

The posseman took the money and closed the front door on his way out.

The prisoners were dragging spurs and belt

173

buckles across the steel bars of their cells. Castleton ignored it. When the vaqueros returned with food, they would be fed.

A dumpy, nondescript-looking man who wore a massive gold chain across the lower part of his vest walked in and nodded. "I'm Paul Bryan," he told Castleton. "I own the mercantile store in Hermasillo."

Ken pointed to a chair. "I'm Ken Castleton," he said, and got a birdlike nod from the portly older man.

"I know who you are, Mr. Castleton. Before I say what I came over here to say, I'd like an answer to one question. Was Walt Brown really in cahoots with three other men to steal the Miller cattle?"

"Yes sir, he was, Mr. Bryan."

"Can you prove it?"

Instead of answering Ken pulled out the forged bill of sale and held it out. After the merchant had read it, Ken said, "Turn it over. That's Anna Marie Miller's signature. Now compare it with the other signature. They aren't even close to bein' alike, are they?"

Paul Bryan studied both sides of the bill of sale several times, then handed back the paper as he said, "By gawd, I never would have believed it."

Ken folded the paper and put it back in his pocket. He did not say a word as he and the merchant faced one another again, not until Bryan said, "Now then, some of us fellers on the town council met a while ago, and decided that if you had proof the sheriff really did what rumor says he did — and I'm convinced of it now — we would offer you the sheriffing job."

Ken shifted slightly in his chair before replying. "That's real decent of you, Mr. Bryan, an' I do appreciate it, but no thanks. I've never been a lawman and never figure to be one. . . . But you've got one hell of a good man right here in town to take the job."

"Who, Mr. Castleton?"

"Will Clavenger, the blacksmith."

Bryan showed no surprise. Evidently he'd heard this before. He said practically the same thing the café man had said. "Will's a good man. He's got lots of good traits, but you don't know him as well as the rest of us do."

"Mr. Bryan, I know him this well — we rode together, first as enemies, then as friends. He's tough and hard and sensible. But best of all, he's honest. Now let me ask you a question. You want someone who's popular or someone who will uphold the law?"

The merchant toyed with his massive gold chain for a moment, then arose, nodded, and walked back out into the night.

Ken was fighting a losing battle with sleep

when the Miller riders returned, replete and carrying trays of food. Ken held the cell room door for them and returned to his chair.

He heard the profanity as the prisoners were finally being fed, and ignored it. He closed his eyes and thought of something that smelled of violets, or maybe it was some other kind of flower, he wasn't sure because except for admiring flowers he scarcely knew one from the other.

When she'd been sitting her horse out yonder in tree shade she'd been wearing a white blouse and a split doeskin riding skirt of fawn color. She had looked at him as though he were a man, instead of some of the other ways she had looked at him.

He was dozing off again when the riders returned, slammed the cell room door, and exclaimed almost in unison that if he'd allow the prisoners to run for it, they'd enjoy target practice from the middle of the road.

What Ken did not know at the time was that they were serious. Mexicans had a sport called *ley fuga;* men were told that if they could reach a distant point alive they could go free. Not one in a thousand ever reached that point no matter how swift they were.

He smiled and said that if one of them would volunteer to stay in the jailhouse office, he and the others could go into the back room and bed down.

José volunteered, and perhaps because he was a tough, durable individual, he looked the least tired. Ken gave him the job and led the others into a kind of storeroom whose barred door at the back of the building led out into an alley.

They had little trouble finding blankets. Over the years of occupancy several lawmen had appropriated the bedrolls of their prisoners.

Ken was almost asleep under two moth-eaten old blankets when Hernan' said, "She said she wanted to see you after we'd brought them here and locked them up."

Ken opened one eye. "If the angel Gabriel was waitin' outside with a golden chariot, he'd have to wait until morning. Go to sleep, Hernan'."

CHAPTER 13

The FM Yard

The vaqueros were still having breakfast at the glum man's café when Ken rode up Main Street. He had eaten early, had shaved and put on a new shirt and trousers he'd got from the general store — the first customer of the day.

What he'd also wanted to do, give two bits to the barber for a chunk of soap and a towel and the use of the barber's bathhouse out back, he hadn't been able to do because there were three men ahead of him.

Being rested and fed made a difference. He had hired a livery horse so his leggy thoroughbred could recover fully from his recent hard use. The horse was barn-sour. After four attempts to bluff his rider so he could return to his corral, the horse lined out, satisfied that, this time anyway, he wouldn't be able to win.

Otherwise, he was a good, solid animal, a little short-backed, which made being astride him in a lope not unlike riding a springless buggy over a washboard road, but having decided that in order to avoid another roweling he would obey his rider, the horse went along very well.

Even when he flushed a band of prairie chickens in the damp morning grass, and they scattered making a noise like a threshing machine, the horse neither shied nor seemed to notice what in most other horses would have resulted, at the very least, in a violent sideward shying jump.

When Ken had the big FM yard in sight, he dropped down to a slogging walk. His mount's interest quickened, probably because he scented other horses.

Chet was choring down at the barn and did not see Castleton until he swung off out front and made the livery horse fast.

Chet came forward smiling, leaned on his hay fork, and said, "She expected you last night. We set up with her until she got mad because you hadn't showed up, and went to bed."

Ken shrugged. "Too tired. Did you explain everything to her?"

"Yep. From start to finish. She was a little mad at me for sneakin' off to find you in the night."

Ken leaned beside his horse on the hitching

rack. "Partner," he said thoughtfully, "that woman's got a disposition like a bear with a sore behind."

Betsy appeared on the distant veranda and called. Ken turned, called back a greeting, then leaned down again facing Betsy's brother as he said, "We got to go after those damned cattle or they'll be spread far and wide."

Chet nodded as his sister called again, this time inviting Ken Castleton to breakfast. Both Chet and the mustanger looked surprised. Ken glanced at the position of the sun and called back. "Already ate in town, Betsy. I'll be over directly."

The girl went back inside and Ken continued to lean on the hitching post. Chet said, "She wants to reward you."

"With money?"

"Yes. That's what she said when her and I was riding back yesterday."

Finally, Ken straightened up. "I don't want her money," he told the younger man, and struck out toward the main house.

Betsy held the door for him to enter and smiled warmly. "Anna Marie'll be along directly," she told him, and led him into the parlor. "I'll get you some coffee."

"No thanks, Betsy," he replied. "I've had my share of coffee for one day."

Betsy looked uncertain. She pointed to a big

leather chair. "I'll tell her you're here."

Castleton watched the lovely girl depart and went to stand in front of the big smoke-darkened fireplace and gaze at a painting of a man with bold eyes, a strong chin, and hair that was gray at the temples, which hung above the fireplace.

He turned at the soft sound of someone entering the parlor from a hallway. Anna Marie was wearing her fawn-colored riding skirt, but today she was also wearing a pale tan blouse. He told himself she was beautiful, but to her face he only smiled a little and said, "Good morning," and added a little more. "Yesterday an' the day before were tough on men and horses. I was too tuckered to come out here last night."

She nodded. "I hope that's an apology, Mr. Castleton. We waited up for you until about eleven o'clock."

His smile winked out. "It wasn't an apology — ma'am — it was a statement of fact."

She went to the center of the room before facing him again. "Why is it," she asked, "that every time we meet it's like flint on steel?"

He answered crisply, "You make it that way. You've made it that way since the first time we met."

She looked at him in silence for a moment then asked if he'd like some coffee. He an-

181

swered her about as he'd answered Betsy Conners, adding, "No, thank you. I've never been a very good coffee drinker. I guess I learned to drink coffee too late in life to care much for it."

"Whiskey, then?" she said.

"What time is it?"

"There is a clock on the mantel behind you."

He looked around and back. "Too early for that, too."

". . . Mr. Castleton, I'd like to —"

"Ken, just plain Ken. That's short for Kenneth."

Her gaze hardened a trifle. "Really? All right — Ken — I'd like to show my appreciation for all you've done, which I'm sure wouldn't have turned out as it did except for your — help."

"Interference, ma'am?"

She colored. "No! For your help. I'd like to show my appreciation by giving you something." She drew a sealed envelope from a pocket and held it toward him.

He made no move to accept the envelope, but looked above it into her eyes. "Money?"

"Yes."

"No, thanks, Mrs. Miller. Divide it up between your vaqueros and the lad down at the barn."

"My vaqueros are paid wages, Mr. Castleton."

"Not for puttin' their lives on the line for you the way they did. And the lad might need a grubstake."

"A grubstake? Did he say he was moving on?"

"No, ma'am. But he's a pretty spirited young feller. Workin' for someone like you'd be a strain on anyone."

She placed the envelope on a little table. She needed the moment required to do that to rein in her anger. As she straightened up she said, "Mr. Castleton, now who is making this hard for both of us?"

Ken smiled at her. "Like you said, it's flint on steel. . . . Would you like to start over, an' leave that damned envelope out of it? I'd like that cup of coffee now."

She was turning toward the kitchen when Betsy appeared with two cups of coffee. Both Anna Marie and Ken stared at her. In order to have responded so quickly she had to have been listening, but in fact since there was no door on the opening between the kitchen and the parlor, and neither of the older people had kept their voices down, Betsy could not have avoided hearing every word that passed between them.

After providing their coffee the girl said,

183

"I'm going down to the barn," and left by the front door.

Castleton finally sat down. Anna Marie did the same a short distance away. Castleton was grinning as he stirred the coffee. When he looked up he said, "She's real sensitive, isn't she?"

Anna Marie nodded. "Very," she replied. "I think she's upset."

Ken tasted the coffee.

Anna Marie put her cup and saucer on the little table beside the envelope and pointed. "That's my husband over the mantel. He built up our ranch starting from practically nothing. Thunder Valley Ranch is one of the largest in the entire Conejo countryside." She rested both hands in her lap as she looked straight at Castleton. "I know people did not think sweet, good-natured Anna Marie Miller would be able to hold things together."

"But you did?"

"Yes, but not by being sweet, docile Anna Marie, Mr. Castleton. The episode with Sheriff Brown and his cattle thieves hasn't been my first encounter with the difficulties of succeeding in a man's world. It was the worst, most threatening, but not the first."

Ken drained his cup and settled back in the chair. "So you stopped being docile, sweet Anna Marie Miller."

"I had no choice, Mr. Castleton. When live-stock buyers rode out from town and patron-izingly offered me ridiculously low prices, I told them they had ten minutes to get out of my yard. When some of the men from Hermasillo came out to comfort me during my bereave-ment, and would have moved in —"

"You gave them ten minutes to get out of your yard."

"Yes. What I'm trying to explain is —"

"You don't have to explain anything to me, Mrs. Miller," Ken said, as he stood up. "I've seen things like this before."

She, too, arose. "Mr. Castleton? . . ."

"No thanks, Mrs. Miller. I don't want your money."

"I wasn't going to offer it again. I was going to ask if you would hire on."

He considered her thoughtfully. She was downright beautiful. "You have Hernan', Gregorio, and José. You also have the lad. I'll ride with them to round up and bring back your cattle, the ones that connivin' free grazer had, an' the ones down yonder at that old ranch." He smiled at her. "You don't need another rider."

"Mr. Castleton," she said in a matter-of-fact tone of voice, "for two years I've been holding back the best heifers. By next year they'll start calving. It will nearly double the amount of cattle on the ranch. I will need another rider. Maybe even two more."

He gazed at her a long time before replying. "Mrs. Miller, I sort of had in mind drifting out to California, maybe, or back East somewhere."

"Just drifting, Mr. Castleton?" The way she said that seemed to imply he had disappointed her.

It was Ken's turn to redden. "I've drifted most of my life. I know — settled folks don't understand that. But a man drifts because he's searching for something. I'll know it when I see it."

She abruptly changed the subject. "Where are my vaqueros?"

"Last I saw, they were in town. I expect they'll be along directly. Will Clavenger is minding the prisoners. Seems there might be some folks in Hermasillo who are friendly toward Sheriff Brown. If the Hermasillo town fathers don't do something they hadn't ought to do, I think the blacksmith'll keep order. He won't need your vaqueros, he's got the fellers who rode with Sheriff Brown, and saw him shown up for a rustler, among other things, to help him."

She went to the door and held it open until he'd passed through to the veranda, then she closed the door and looked in the direction of the barn.

"Betsy and her brother like you very much, Mr. Castleton."

"An' I like them very much, Mrs. Miller."

"I worry a little about Chet."

"No need to. As far as I can see, he's found a home an' a job, an' his sister's in good company."

"That's it, Mr. Castleton. If you leave I think he might feel now that his sister has a friend, she won't need him anymore. I think lads his age have a wanderlust."

Ken looked down at her profile. This conversation seemed to have something to it he didn't comprehend. Not until she looked back at him and said, "If you'd stay, he would stay. If you leave and he leaves, it's going to be very hard on Betsy."

Ken wagged his head. "I'm beginnin' to understand you a little, Mrs. Miller." He smiled at her, nodded, and walked down off the veranda toward the barn.

Betsy and her brother were waiting. They had grained and cuffed his livery horse to pass the time until he arrived. Chet spoke first. "You'n her had a fight?"

Ken grinned at them. "No."

"What about the cattle?" Betsy asked. Ken told them he had offered to help bring them all back to their own range, and Betsy looked relieved as her brother asked about the vaqueros. While he was explaining that they were probably still in town, Betsy slipped out of the barn to join Anna Marie on the porch.

She studied the older woman's profile for a moment before saying, "He's going to help drive the cattle back."

Anna Marie nodded and answered rather absently, "I know."

Betsy had a question. "He said you didn't fight, but it sounded to me like you did. Didn't you?"

Anna Marie faced the girl with a soft look in her eyes. "Not exactly . . . fight, honey. We argued a little. He's a . . . he's something I'm not accustomed to."

They both waved from the porch as Ken rode out of the yard in the direction of Hermasillo. He waved back. Chet leaned on the side of the big barn opening also watching.

When the women went inside the house, Chet brought in a horse from the corral and saddled it without haste. He left the yard as he'd done before, by keeping the massive log structure between himself and the main house until he was distant enough to change course and ride toward Hermasillo.

Ken was still a fair distance from Hermasillo when he saw three riders up ahead. They were riding fast, and for that reason he doubted it was Anna Marie's vaqueros.

He stopped, certain they had seen him, and was watching them when a puff of gray appeared, followed by a second puff.

He whirled the livery horse and hooked it hard in the direction from which he had just come. The horse responded gallantly, but he was not in the same class as Ken's thoroughbred who could, when he had to, run a hole in the daylight.

The distance was great enough for Castleton's hired mount to pretty well assure that it and its rider would reach the Miller yard before the three hard-riding men in pursuit got too close. Ken alternately looked back, and wondered who in the hell they were.

To alert the people in the yard trouble was on the way, he fired his six-gun into the air, then twisted from the waist and emptied the gun in the direction of his pursuers, knowing very well the distance was too great to hope for a hit. But his explosive defiance did one thing, the three hard-riders slackened off a little, dropped to a trot and kept coming, evidently unwilling to get any closer, which enabled Ken to race into the yard, enter the barn before dismounting and to reload his handgun before putting the winded livery horse into a stall.

Anna Marie was on the porch with Betsy when he came out of the barn. He yelled at them to get inside and bar the doors. He pointed to the oncoming horsemen.

They obeyed without a single question, which, had Ken been less preoccupied, might have made him marvel. Women usually asked questions before they moved.

The riders suddenly yanked to a sliding halt looking back. Ken did not see the solitary horseman behind them until the riders separated a little. He saw him, recognized him, and his heart sank.

Chet Conners!

One of the riders raised his six-gun, took deliberate aim, and fired. Ken heard the delayed muzzle blast and held his breath. Six-guns were not noted for accuracy if distance was involved. Chet seemed to flinch a little to the right, halted, dismounted, and knelt. That was the indication to both the riders and Ken Castleton that the youth had a carbine.

The riders lost interest in Ken and scattered as Chet fired, waited a moment, then fired again. He missed both times. Running horses are hard to hit even from a kneeling position.

The riders also had Winchesters. Ken could see sunlight glinting off butt plates, but they did not stop fleeing to fight back, which favored young Conners, who sprang back astride his horse and made a belly-down run for the yard.

CHAPTER 14

Surprise!

Chet only looked back once — that was when someone fired a carbine. He had no idea where the bullet went and swung forward in a low crouch to thunder into the yard, dismount on the fly, and lead his animal into the barn.

Ken took the lad's reins, told him to keep watch, and went deeper into the old structure to care for the horse. When he returned Chet was down on one knee with his carbine in both hands. When Ken asked who they were, the lad's reply shocked him.

"That long-nosed bastard named Fincher, the 'breed Indian, and the feller with the red hair."

"You're sure?"

Chet left off watching the land beyond the yard to scowl at Castleton. "I'm sure. I was parallel to you north of the big brush patch an' got a good look at 'em when you stopped. It was Fincher that fired at you."

Ken leaned upon the opposite side of the

opening, waiting for the gunmen to reappear. There was no sign of them. He called to young Conners. "If it's them, then they broke out of the Hermasillo jailhouse."

Chet knew nothing about that and right at this moment was not concerned. He reiterated what he'd said before. "It's them three. I don't know how they broke out, but I saw each one of them real good as they stopped to shoot at you."

Ken growled under his breath. "Son of a bitch." He recalled his conversation with Will Clavenger. He'd have bet a new hat Fincher, the half-breed, and the redheaded man would never get past the blacksmith. In broad daylight, he told himself, and turned back to studying the empty land.

They hadn't emerged from the brush patch. Ken caught his breath and went swiftly to the rear barn opening, half expecting to see the rustlers sneaking up out there. There was no sign of them, but they'd hardly had enough time to get around behind the barn on foot.

He remained back there as he called forward. "Any sign of 'em, Chet?"

"No. Maybe they're palavering. Maybe they decided to head off in a different direction. With us forted up in here, they got to figure the odds ain't too great in their favor."

Ken checked his reloaded handgun, listened

193

for the faintest sound, and risked leaning out to look along the back of the barn and the more distant wagon shed.

Ken ducked back out of sight. If Fincher had broken out of the Hermasillo jail, there must have been a fight, and that being the case, Fincher would know riders from town were on his trail.

Maybe he would head out in a different direction, but it sure as hell wouldn't be west where he'd be in sight, and not northward either, because beyond the brush patch was open, rolling grassland where three horsemen would stick up like a sore thumb.

He and Chet had an hour of waiting that seemed like a year. The sun began to slant away and cast weak shadows. The yard and the land beyond it was deathly quiet.

They spent it puzzling over the apparent jailbreak, and the lack of a pursuing posse of townsmen. By then, if there was pursuit, it should have showed up, and the eastward range shone with sunshine without movement or dust.

Chet said, "Where is the sheriff? Maybe he didn't break out with them."

Ken went to look out and around before coming back to say, "He'd have come with them if he could. He sure didn't have any reason to want to stay in town."

That added to the mystery.

The horses needed water and the stone trough out back was nearer the corrals than to the barn. Ken took the livery horse to the rear of the barn, got on his left side, and let him tug the shank when he smelled water.

Ken stretched across the animal's back. They had to be out there somewhere. Unless they'd decided getting revenge wouldn't be worth it, and had indeed headed off in a different direction.

His assessment of Pete Fincher was that he was a mean, vindictive individual. If he had come out here after escaping from jail when a less hate-motived man would have headed due south or maybe even northward toward the timbered uplands, he would not be riding away from the yard now.

Ken was right.

Chet had been up front keeping vigil for only a few minutes when he called to Ken. "What does that mean?" he asked. As soon as Ken saw the white dish towel suspended from a broom handle on the veranda, he swore. "It means that son of a bitch didn't ride off. It means while we were standin' in here trying to figure out where he was, he snuck down one of the gullies to the south and came up behind the house. He's in there now."

Chet's grip on the carbine showed white knuckles. His sister was over there. Fincher had already shown that he wanted her.

"I'll kill him," the youth said quietly.

Ken growled at him. "You step out of here and it'll be the other way around. Stay on your side of the doorway and keep watch. I'm going to holler to them. The white flag means they want to palaver."

Ken leaned slightly on the opposite side of the barn entrance and yelled, "There's nothing to talk about, Fincher."

The reply came almost instantly. "There's lots to talk about, Castleton. We got two real pretty ladies an' we got a trade to offer you. You listening?"

"I'm listening," Ken replied.

"We got Walt Brown's cache money. He died in his cell after he told us where the cache was. An' we just found two thousand dollars in Miz Miller's safe. Now then — you and that young feller pitch out your guns and walk out where we can see you. Where we can keep an eye on you while we get a-horseback . . . Castleton? We don't have a hell of a lot of time."

Ken did not look around or he would have seen a very white face across the way. He spat, leaned back, and thought. It was his mistake that had allowed them to get into the house, but that was water under the bridge.

Chet broke into his thoughts by announcing that he was going to pitch his weapons away and walk out of the barn.

"They'll drop you in your tracks," Ken said. "If he'd said to turn our horses loose an' run them off, I might have thought he don't figure to kill us both."

Chet stared in the direction of the main house. "My sister . . ." he said.

Ken was less brusque this time when he addressed the younger man. "Your sister and Anna Marie Miller is all they got to trade with. For now I think they're safe."

Chet groaned.

"Use your head," Ken told him. "You won't be any good to your sister if they shoot you, an' they sure as hell will."

He shouted back across the yard, "Fincher! You got to do better'n that."

The response was loud. "The women, Castleton. The damned women!"

Ken hung fire for a long moment. He could see no way out, but he made one last effort. "Fincher! Send one of your men down to the barn unarmed. We'll keep him to make sure you do as you said — ride away. . . . Fincher, take the damned money with you."

This time the reply was much longer in

coming, time Ken used to look around at young Conners. The youth's eyes were fixed almost hypnotically on the main house. He was as tense as a spring. Ken told him to relax, as long as the bickering was in progress the outlaws would have something more important for them to think about than his sister.

Chet's reply to that was as he'd said before in the same icy tone of voice, "I'll kill him. I'll kill all three of them."

Ken nodded. "But not just yet," and faced around as Pete Fincher's delayed response came back. "We don't make no trades with you, Castleton. It's the other way around — an' you'd better do like I said, we're wastin' time."

"Walk out of here an' get shot?"

"I told you, throw out the weapons and walk out where we can keep an eye on you until we ride off. No one's goin' to shoot you. You got my word on that."

Ken scorned questioning the outlaw's word out loud.

He said nothing for a long while. Chet finally crossed over to where Ken was standing and put aside his Winchester, drew his handgun without haste, and pointed it at Ken. "We don't do what they say an' they'll kill my sister an' Miz Miller."

Ken looked from the uncocked gun to the

198

youth's face, and swung. The blow sent Chet's hat sailing like a wounded bird. Chet's six-gun spun across the barn floor as the youth crumpled.

That woodpecker was back, hammering on the back of the wagon shed. That was the only sound, but as Ken picked up Chet's six-gun and shoved it into his waistband, Fincher called again. "This is your last chance, Castleton. We're goin' to shove Miz Miller out front where you can watch, and kill her."

Ken responded tartly. "Why didn't you head up into the mountains, why come back here?"

"To settle with Miz Miller an' you."

"You took one hell of a risk, Fincher."

"We got two thousand more dollars, an' that makes a little delay worthwhile. Now — you an' the young feller toss out your weapons. You got a few seconds to make up your minds, I'm through talkin' to you."

Ken turned to look down. Chet was staring toward the back of the barn, lips parted. Ken turned fully as a soft voice said, "The town was in an uproar," and Hernan' Iturbide grinned widely. "They was screaming for a posse when we left. They was pointing up the north road, but we did not go that way because we wanted to get home."

"How did you know they were in the main

house?" Ken asked.

José came into the barn opening beside the *mayordomo*. "The white flag on the veranda." Gregorio came up, too, his aimlessly drifting eye making its slow circle. "We rode north for two miles, maybe, then came back southward keeping the barn between us and them. Our horses are tied on the north side of the wagon shed. *Señor*, if you can keep him talking I think we can get behind the house. We saw their horses tied back there."

Fincher yelled again. "Castleton! She's comin' out!" Moments later the front door opened and Anna Marie was shoved through as the door was slammed behind her.

Ken nodded to Hernan'. "Set them afoot if you can." The vaqueros faded from sight along the south side of the log barn. There was the bunkhouse, the springhouse, and what seemed to be a storehouse or cold room because it was not built of wood, it was made of rock.

There were spaces between these structures of something like fifteen feet. Men would be exposed crossing those spaces on their way toward the west side of the main house. If it had been later in the afternoon, or even dusk, the risk would have been much less, but whatever delay Castleton could conjure would never be allowed to last that long.

Chet got up feeling his swelling jaw. Ken handed him back his six-gun and pointed to the Winchester. As the youth went to retrieve it, Ken said, "Mrs. Miller's on the porch. And partner, don't never point an uncocked gun."

Chet went forward to look, and sucked down a rattling breath. "It's not just her," he said. "There's a gun muzzle aimed from inside the house at her back."

Ken nodded. "That's the gun they'll use to shoot us with the moment we walk out of here."

"What can we do?"

Ken shouted across the yard without answering the youth. "Fincher, got a better trade for you."

"I told you, I'm through talkin'. Either you fellers come out where we can see you or the lady gets shot in the back!"

"The offer," Ken retorted as though Fincher's voice hadn't rung with finality, "is — you take the lady back inside an' we'll come out."

There was a furious discussion among the outlaws in the main house. Fincher stood like stone letting their protests of wasting more time break over him like smoke. "I want that son of a bitch, Castleton," he said.

"How long you expect it'll be before them

fellers in town'll go up the north road until they see where we cut off in this direction?" Lytle said. "Damn it, you can come back and settle with Castleton later. Right now the only thing in our favor is gettin' the hell away from here an' stayin' in front of whoever's comin' after us."

Tom, the half-breed Indian, said he was going to leave whether Fincher came along or not.

During the lull in their argument every one of them heard running horses, and the half-breed swore as he ran toward the rear of the house.

Fincher's narrowed eyes widened. He, too, ran toward the back of the house. Only the redheaded rustler remained in the parlor. He turned when an unsteady and slightly breathless voice told him to drop his six-gun.

He turned, and the beautiful girl was standing in the hallway entrance pointing a big-bored belly-gun at him. It was at full cock.

John Lytle dropped his weapon and sneered. "You damned idiot," he said to Betsy, as loud voices came from somewhere out back. "You pull that trigger, girlie, an' you'll think the sky fell on you."

Betsy squeezed the trigger.

The sound was thunderous inside the house. The yelling men out back became instantly silent. Fincher called out. "John, was that you?"

Lytle was face down and dead.

"John, damn it, *was that you?*"

Betsy dropped her derringer and fled down the hallway to her room, barred the door from the inside, and went swiftly to raise the window. She was white as a ghost and shaking, but she managed to climb out and drop to the ground as someone yelled, "They got our horses!"

Fincher and Tom came cautiously to the doorway leading into the parlor and saw their dead companion. There was blood showing, but not very much. Betsy's slug had hit Lytle squarely in the center of the breastbone.

Tom muttered at Fincher, "They got inside."

Fincher scoffed. "They're both still in the damned barn. I'll go call down there an' you'll see."

As Fincher stepped around the corpse and cracked the door, he got his second stunning surprise. Anna Marie Miller was no longer on the veranda.

He closed and barred the door as the half-breed came up. "Get her back in here, Tom. We need her more'n ever."

"She's not out there."

Tom shouldered Fincher aside, opened the

door a crack, and looked. The veranda was empty except for two chairs and a little cross-legged handmade table.

The half-breed closed the door, dropped the *tranca* into its hangers, one on each side of the door, and stood gazing at Pete Fincher. "Call," he told Fincher. "They ain't still in the barn. Go ahead, call down there."

Fincher stepped to the door, opened it a crack, and sang out. "Castleton?"

Ken answered. "Yeah. You goin' to send one of them out to guarantee our safety when we leave the barn?"

"Castleton, make the lad show himself."

"Like hell!"

"Well, tell him to yell out."

Ken nodded and Chet called in a loud, but unmistakably youthful voice. "Fincher, if you harm my sister I'll spend the rest of my life hunting you."

Fincher closed and rebarred the door and stood with his back to it. Across the parlor near the hallway entrance the half-breed was turning something over in his hand. Fincher asked where he had found the little gun and the half-breed pointed to the hallway entrance.

Fincher ripped out a savage curse and went past Tom with a lunging stride. He stopped in front of Betsy's door and hammered on it.

The door did not yield and there was no response to his knocking. From behind Fincher, Tom said, "Kick it open. She's in there."

There was no way to kick the oaken panel open as long as the *tranca* was in place behind it, but Fincher was not without experience in opening barred doors. He went to the kitchen and returned with a long-bladed carving knife, which he inserted into the crack between the door and the sash, and worked it upwards until he could feel heavy wood against the blade. He moved it up very slowly. When his hand was almost to the top of the door the *tranca* swung over and Fincher opened the door.

Tom had his gun cocked as he pushed past Fincher. He turned slowly around and back. With a blank look he said, "She ain't here."

Fincher pointed to the open window.

Tom went over there, leaned out and looked in both directions. He lingered until Fincher walked over and shouldered him aside to also lean out and look. Not only was there no sign of the girl, but in the southward distance he could see their three horses running free, heads up and tails waving.

Tom holstered his weapon and stood staring at Pete Fincher. "On foot," he said. "John's dead, an' it can't just be them two in the barn. Now what do we do?"

205

Fincher went back to the parlor and looked out a window. There was no sign of life at the barn, but he could not see inside.

CHAPTER 15

Desperate Men

Gregorio smiled as he, José, and Hernan' led the women into the barn. Betsy ran into her brother's arms.

Hernan' and his companions went up to the front of the barn to spy on the main house. It was too quiet. José said, "If they ran out, where can they go on foot?"

There were many places they could go; hiding places were everywhere. Hernan' did not answer José's question. He knew every inch of the yard, and every corner of the buildings.

"Rats," he eventually murmured in Spanish. "Like rats they will find a place."

José replied curtly, also in Spanish. "Then find them we will."

Hernan' looked at the dark, powerfully built man. "How, companion, by showing your face?"

José said nothing. Fincher and Tom were more dangerous now than they had been before. Once, they'd had horses to flee on. Now, they had no way to flee; they had to shoot their way out of their predicament.

José remained at the front of the barn while Hernan' returned to the others. Betsy was crying her heart out in Anna Marie's arms. She had told them of shooting the one named Lytle.

Ken went out back, not expecting to see anything, and didn't see anything. The sun was reddening on its slide toward beyond the horizon. Several corralled horses were lined up like crows on a fence staring at the back of the barn. It was close to chore time.

That would have to wait.

Ken returned to the others. "They can wait us out until dark," he said.

Anna Marie replied shortly, "Let them go. It's not worth getting killed."

Chet had a question. "Where are the men from town? If a posse was on the way, they've had time enough."

Pete Fincher went back to the parlor, gazed in the direction of the barn, and said, "Her damned vaqueros must have got the girl. It had to be. If it'd been riders from town they'd have charged in here and made a fight out of it."

Tom said nothing.

Fincher finally turned his back on the front

window and said, "Let's get out of here."

This time the half-breed said, "Go where? Without horses they can hunt us down. At least we got cover in here."

Fincher was irritable. "Yeah, we got walls, an' sooner or later they'll surround the damned house. Come along."

They returned to Betsy's bedroom, looked around past the open window, and dropped to the ground along the back of the house. The hunters had become the hunted.

There was no sign of their horses across the vast expanse of southward open country. They crept to the east end of the house, slipped down the north side, and got into shadows where they had a clear view of the log barn and the horses out back in the corral waiting to be fed.

It was the horses that held their interest longest. Fincher said, "Tom, maybe after dark —"

The half-breed was a practical man. "By then the yard'll be full of men from town."

"All right, then you tell me — how do we get those horses!"

Tom went back along the east side of the house and waited until Fincher joined him, then said, "We shouldn't have shoved the woman outside. If we still had her we could trade her for horses."

Fincher scowled. "If," he said harshly. "If ain't goin' to help us now."

Tom nodded about that. "The vaqueros had to get around back to run off our horses by usin' them buildings over yonder. What'd be wrong with us doin' the same thing?"

"A barn full of men with guns," replied Fincher in the same harsh tone.

Tom leaned on the wall and looked steadily at Pete Fincher. "You want to give up?" he asked. "If they don't kill us we'll spend the rest of our lives in prison. I had a cousin who died in prison. I'm not going to do that." As he pushed off the wall Tom continued to stare at Fincher as he said, "You stay here, maybe make them think we're both over here. I'm goin' to sneak around them outbuildings like they done. We got to have two horses."

Fincher said nothing as he watched Tom go back toward the rear of the house, but as soon as he was no longer in sight, Fincher shook his head. The idea of getting two horses was fine, but actually getting them would be just about impossible.

For one thing the corrals were directly behind the barn, so anyone inside the barn could see someone near the corrals. For another thing, the people inside the barn would surely have someone watching the country behind the barn as well as the front.

Fincher liked the idea of being alone. He had the money from Sheriff Brown's cache and the two thousand from the Miller office in a money belt under his shirt. The original agreement was to divide it equally once the three rustlers were safely away. Now, with John Lytle dead and Tom gone, Fincher had to worry only about himself. At least, he had all the money.

He returned to the corner of the house and stood in shade watching the barn. He decided he would go along the rear of the house until he could see down there, and turned back.

At the southeast corner he halted, waited, then peered around. He did not feel desperate, although he told himself he probably should. His life had been a long series of narrow escapes, pursuits, and shootouts. He could not recollect ever living any other way. It had sharpened his wits, made him cruel and ruthless.

As he stood near the southwest corner of the main house and paused to listen before peeking out, he felt no fear. As long as he was able to move and hold a weapon, he had no reason to fear.

There was no sign of Tom. Shadows were creeping out, the red sun was steadily sinking, and Fincher had a sudden feeling that he and Tom might get clear. If not with Tom, then he would get away alone.

Three horses were standing side by side at the point of the corrals nearest the barn, mutely staring. Fincher smiled. Hungry horses were more alert than fed ones.

He saw Tom crawling around the far side of the corrals. Fincher continued to smile. That was what had first got Tom into trouble: stealing horses. He'd stolen quite a few before being caught. Now, with Fincher watching, the half-breed was crawling a yard at a time toward the far side of the corrals, visible only when he moved, otherwise he blended perfectly with the earth and grass.

The lined-up horses were not aware of his presence behind them, not even when he glided under the lowest corral poles.

Fincher was fixed in place, scarcely breathing, as he watched. Tom was good, damned good.

The gate opened with scarcely a sound. One horse turned, watched the gate swing open, and seemed unable to decide whether to make a run for freedom or wait to be fed.

Fincher watched that one horse as Tom continued to crawl until he was beyond the corrals back in the grass. It had been a perfect example of how an experienced horse thief operated.

That horse finally made a decision. He

turned, eyed the gate, saw something crawling away beyond the corral, and whirled.

The moment he broke away the other two horses turned, saw him go out the gate, shy from something to his right, and run steadily away. They followed his example.

The sound of the running horses brought Ken to the rear doorway, as the horses put distance between themselves and the yard.

The three vaqueros stood beside Ken. Hernan' wasted no time. He called for the others to follow him and went running toward the far side of the wagon shed.

Fincher watched all this from his point of vantage. He could probably have hit at least one of the running men if he'd cared to, but he stood with both thumbs hooked in his cartridge belt watching.

He saw the vaqueros break away in pursuit of the running loose stock and smiled. Now, with Tom undetected behind the barn, and he himself able to see any further attempt of those still in the barn to also go in pursuit, he waited.

But no one emerged from the barn. Chet would have but Ken caught his arm and held him back. Anna Marie was with Betsy. She started forward as Ken drove Betsy's brother deeper into the barn. She read Ken's expression correctly and said nothing.

They were not afoot, there were still three horses in stalls, Ken's short-backed buckskin livery animal, Chet's horse, and the handsome animal with the flaxen mane and tail that belonged to Anna Marie.

Ken left Chet with the women and returned to the rear of the barn. He saw the open gate, knew it had been closed before, and stood just inside the barn in the dark shadows looking for a man, or for movement. He saw neither, although Tom was pressed flat against the ground, absolutely motionless and hidden by tall grass.

Ken turned, looked back where the others were watching him, and said, "That was very good. I don't know how they did it, but that gate was closed the last time I looked out here." He turned back watching for movement. As before, there was none.

Anna Marie came up beside him. She watched her riders growing small in the distance as they spread out in pursuit of the escaping horses, and sighed.

Ken looked at her profile. She looked tired, there were dark circles under her eyes. He reached, took her hand in his and squeezed. She did not squeeze back, but as she freed her fingers she said, "Let them go, Ken. Tell them we'll give them horses and they can go.

It's just not worth all this."

He returned her gaze for a moment before slightly shaking his head. "It won't be that easy. They didn't hurt as much by stampeding those horses, an' I wish Hernan' hadn't gone after them — because sure as hell that's what they want. To thin us out in the barn. To separate us."

She looked steadily at him. "Where will it end?"

"Right now," he told her, "we're back where we were. Chet an' me against the two that are left. Except that now they got nothin' to trade with. That leaves 'em with no choice but to settle up real quick, before your riders get back."

Pete Fincher was still watching from the corner of the main house when Tom reached him, coming from behind Fincher. He was sweaty, soiled, and smiling for the first time in several days. Fincher, who was a man rarely given to compliments, said, "Damn good, Tom. I don't know anyone who could've done better."

Tom was already thinking past his triumph. "The vaqueros are gone. That leaves the kid, the woman, an' Castleton. Pete, you stay here while I go around to the other side. When I fire into the barn you duck down behind them buildings I used, and try to get close to the rear doorway."

Fincher gazed at his companion. This was the first time since they had been acquainted that Tom had shown any ability toward strategy. Under less desperate circumstances Fincher might have snarled about Tom usurping his position as leader. Now, he nodded in agreement and turned to watch Tom hurry along the rear of the main house. When Tom turned down the west wall where he would be able to see into the barn, not completely but well enough, Fincher drew his handgun, checked its chamber, and waited.

In the distance the vaqueros were rounding ahead of the fleeing loose stock, preparing to turn them back. There would not be much time.

A gunshot sounded from the opposite side of the main house, followed by another shot.

Fincher darted to the back stone wall of the nearest outbuilding where he could be seen by anyone looking in his direction from the rear barn opening. Another gunshot sounded. Fincher darted to the next building, nearly tripped over a washbasin someone had neglected to hang back on its nail, swore to himself, and flattened himself against the wall, gun up and cocked. No one appeared in the rear of the barn.

Tom fired again, another slanting shot that struck wood midway inside the barn on the north side where the people on the south side saw the wood splinter.

Ken told Chet to go watch out back. Whoever was firing into the barn had to be over by the main house where he could not see directly into the barn. As Chet turned to obey, Anna Marie reached out to brush Ken's arm with her fingers.

He shook her hand away. "He's not trying to hit any of us, Anna Marie, he's shooting to keep our attention out front."

She turned as Chet strained to look southward. He saw a shadowy silhouette dart from behind the bunkhouse in the direction of the next outbuilding, the last one before the barn could be reached. Chet raised his right arm and fired. The silhouette leapt around the side of the outbuilding where Chet could not see him.

Another of those ranging shots came from the direction of the main house, then there was a long pause, which Ken thought was being used by the shooter over there to reload. He risked stepping forward to seek gun smoke. What he saw was enough smoke to indicate the gunman was over at the southeast corner of the house.

When Chet fired Ken swung around. Anna

Marie was comforting Betsy again, holding the girl's face against her shoulder.

Ken called to young Conners. Chet called back. "There's someone sneakin' down this way."

"Be careful," Ken yelled. "Don't show yourself."

Chet stepped deeper into barn gloom and waited.

Fincher was doing the same thing, waiting. That he had been seen bothered him. Those vaqueros returning with the loose stock would hear the gunfire, mount the loose stock, and come riding hell for leather.

He looked out there, saw them, and abandoned the plan of trying to flank the people in the barn and get back to the safety of the main house. He ran like a deer and made it as far as the little stone building where he paused very briefly to look back.

There was no one looking his way from the rear of the barn, but he distinctly heard the shout of the vaqueros. It inspired him to make a final race for the protection of the main house.

He made it, flattened himself along the rear of the house at the southwest corner, the same place he'd left shortly before, and this time he felt real anxiety as his lungs pumped from unaccustomed exertion.

Tom fired one last round into the barn before he glimpsed the racing figure of Fincher retreating. He went down the rear of the house until he and Fincher met. There, Tom said, "What'n hell did you give up for? We could've had 'em."

"Didn't you see her riders leave the loose horses and come helling it back?"

Tom's answer was short. "Sure I saw them, an' if you'd just got inside that damned barn, we'd have had the women an' maybe Castleton to trade 'em for horses."

They were staring at each other when they heard someone shout something in Spanish. They had no idea what the vaquero had said, but they had no trouble hearing a horse coming in their direction at a run.

CHAPTER 16

Cornered!

At the very last moment something screamed a silent warning to José. He hauled back, his horse had to rear and slide before he could change from a run to a trot, and momentum carried him to the corner of the house where Fincher and Tom were waiting, guns drawn.

They saw each other at the last moment. José had his six-gun lightly held in his right hand, but in order to fire it he had to swing the gun across in front of his saddle horn while the two strained faces staring at him had no such obstacle. Fincher fired too quickly. Tom was steadier. He and José fired at the same time.

Tom went over backwards under impact and José was nearly lifted from his saddle before falling. The horse, terrified by gunfire, would have fled except that Fincher grabbed its flying reins.

At the front of the barn Ken and Hernan' watched, unable to do a thing. They saw José get shot out of his saddle, saw someone over there struggling to get close enough to mount, and saw the rider make a flying mount and rein savagely eastward so that the house would protect his back.

It happened too fast for the people in the barn to understand anything except that there had been three gunshots. By the time Gregorio got up beside Ken, only the echoes of a running horse somewhere behind the house traveling in a southerly direction indicated that someone had escaped.

Ken said, "Fincher, the son of a bitch!"

Hernan' yelled at Gregorio. They both raced toward their companion who had not moved since landing face down on the ground. If they thought there might still be a killer over there, they gave no indication of it.

Ken turned swiftly, led the short-backed horse out, and flung a saddle on him. His mind told him that the horse Fincher had taken had already been run hard before the vaqueros reached the yard. He could not keep that up much longer.

Chet watched briefly, then went after another horse. He was saddling when Ken sprang up and rode out of the barn by the rear opening. Betsy cried out to him and even Anna Marie told him to stay with them. It was his sister's cry that made her brother hesitate, and in that moment Hernan' came running back, saw the saddled horse, shunted Chet aside, sprang up, and also left the barn by the rear opening. Chet stood like a stone watching his horse, his bridle, and his booted carbine disappear.

Gregorio appeared in the front barn door with José in his arms like a child.

They were both splashed with blood. Anna Marie pointed to a place where Gregorio could place him, and spread canvas on the ground. Gregorio removed his old hat and clutched it as Anna Marie opened José's shirt. She had her back to Gregorio and did not move for a long time, then she twisted, looked up, and gently shook her head. José Elizondo was dead.

Gregorio's eyes brimmed, his mouth pulled flat to conceal his torment, and he went over and sank down beside Betsy. She put an arm around his shoulders.

It was so still inside the barn that they could faintly hear a running horse. Hernan' had Ken in sight but Pete Fincher was so far ahead he appeared only as a moving blur.

Hernan' was a lifelong horseman. He knew, for instance, that he would not have to run his horse until it was wind-broken, because Fincher was on the verge of doing that to José's horse.

He was more interested in the long stride and easy motion of Castleton's mount, who left Hernan' steadily farther and farther back.

Hernan' slackened to a trot and rode steadily at that gait; that he was being left farther back by the minute did not trouble him. As a horseman, he knew Castleton would overtake Fincher in time, and perhaps by the time Hernan' overtook them, Castleton would have killed Fincher.

If Fincher wasn't already dead, Hernan' would kill him.

Once, the *mayordomo* twisted to look back. A party of riders was raising dust from the north on their way to the ranch yard. He smiled bitterly. If they had arrived an hour earlier José would probably still be alive.

It happened sooner than either of Fincher's pursuers expected; the fleeing rustler's horse suddenly stumbled, tried to recover, and went down in an upended sprawl.

Fincher landed on his feet and looked back. He had seen that stocky livery horse before.

There was no cover worth the name, but a mud and stone jacal was about half a mile ahead on Fincher's left. He raced hard to reach it before the pursuer got into firing range.

The jacal was, like many of them, one fairly large room with a beehive fireplace in one corner. There were two windows and a sagging old door held up by shriveled leather hinges. Neither of the windows had glass in them but there were brittle fragments of scraped paper-thin rawhide that, when someone had resided here, had allowed warmth to come in, and also prevented anyone inside from looking out.

In earlier times it was this inability to see through paper-thin rawhide that had allowed bloody-handed marauders to creep up the walls of jacals and kill their inhabitants.

Fincher finally knew fear. He was breathing hard as he sprang past the door, gun up and ready although he had not believed anyone lived here before he got close.

Several wood rats half as large as cats leapt out the paneless windows squeaking in terror.

There was evidence that the jacal had not been lived in for many years. In the firebox of the corner cooking and heating place there was a wood rat nest nearly filling the entire cooking area. If its owner was over there, he was deep in his jumble of twigs being very still.

Fincher looked out the window in the west wall, saw Castleton approaching without haste, and would right at that moment have traded half the wealth in his money belt for a rifle, or even a carbine.

Instinct told him that this was the end of

the trail for someone, either him or Ken Castleton. He saw another rider in the distance but only watched him briefly. Castleton was what mattered.

• The sun was low, red as blood and flashing its last rays in a sweeping flood of light. Shadows were everywhere, although this far south of the Miller yard there was less brush than there had been northward. There were a few scraggly trees, including several lacy paloverdes.

The range down here did not appear to have been grazed over at all. In places it brushed the underside of Castleton's stirrups.

Ken watched the horse Fincher had been riding get unsteadily to its feet, look around with bloodshot eyes, and could have shot Fincher for what he'd done to the animal, if for no other reason. The horse staggered in the direction of a gnarled old tree and stood over there in a head-hung stance. If it wasn't wind-broken, Ken thought as he reined to a stop, it would be a damned miracle.

He was far enough north of the jacal not to be in pistol range, and he hadn't seen a boot on José's saddle, which meant Fincher did not have a saddle gun.

He dismounted and called ahead. In the clear late-day air, as still as the grave, his words carried perfectly.

"Fincher! Come out! Leave your gun inside and come out of there."

His words echoed. There was no answer. He tried again. "Fincher! You're all that's left! Come out!"

There still was no reply.

Ken raised his six-gun, aimed steadily at the front window, and fired. The echo this time was loud and lingering. Ken lowered the gun to watch, but there was no sign of movement either inside the hut or outside it.

"Fincher! Others'll be along. If you make a fight out of it you're goin' to look like a sieve."

This time there was answer. "I'll look like one anyway. You want to come in here an' get me — come on!"

Ken glanced around, saw Hernan' approaching, saw the *mayordomo*'s booted Winchester and called again. "The longer you put this off the less chance you have."

"Castleton, you bastard, I don't have no chance, anyway," Fincher called back. "Come on, try an' get over here!"

A moment later Fincher called again, this time in a slightly different tone of voice. "What's your price, Castleton? Quick, before that Mexican gets down here."

"How much you got, Fincher? How much you willing to give to get out there an' be on your way?"

"Two thousand in greenbacks."

"Not enough, Fincher. Try again."

"You idiot, that vaquero'll be close enough to hear us directly. Four thousand, an' that's it."

"You don't have four thousand, Fincher."

"The hell I don't. I got two thousand from the Miller place an' I got another two thousand from Sheriff Brown's cache in Hermasillo."

"Before you shot him?"

"Yeah. Castleton, that Mex is gettin' —"

"Never mind him," Ken called back. "Did you shoot Sheriff Brown in his cell?"

"Yes, damn it, yes. Right after he told us where his cache was."

"Where'd you get the gun?"

"Castleton, for chrissake, that Mexican —"

"Where did you get the gun, Fincher?"

"Sheriff Brown give us all guns. Some feller I never saw before snuck them in to him. The same feller knocked the blacksmith over the head. I guess the blacksmith knew the feller who snuck in the guns because he let him come down into the cell room while he stayed back in the office. After he gave Sheriff Brown the guns he went back up front, got behind the blacksmith, and knocked him over the head. He give us the keys and we went out the back way, down the livery barn, got horses and . . . Castleton, that Mexican's close enough to hear

227

us. Four thousand dollars. We'll have to leave the Mexican face down or you got to divvy up with him."

Ken was in no hurry to conclude this exchange. He could hear Hernan' finally. "Fincher? How much you got?"

"Four thousand dollars."

"I didn't come down in the last rain. You only got a hundred dollars a head for those prime Miller cattle?"

For a long moment Pete Fincher was silent. He probably had to wrestle with himself because, as before, the longer this situation went on, the worse off it was going to be for him and he wanted to live.

"Six thousand, Castleton. That's every dime I got for the cattle an' from the Miller place. I got it in a belt under my shirt. You lead that horse over here an' I'll toss you the money belt."

Ken laughed. "You'll hand me a slug an' get away with your six thousand, Fincher."

"I swear to God . . . All right, I'll pitch the belt out now."

"And your gun."

Fincher swore. "I got to have the gun, Castleton. I'll throw the money belt out an' you lead your horse over an' stay on his off side with your gun across the seat of the saddle. . . . Castleton?"

Ken turned, watched Hernan' drop from a lope to a walk, and waved. The *mayordomo* waved back.

"Castleton! Gawddammit!"

Hernan' rode up and swung to the ground eyeing the jacal. In an almost disinterested way he asked if Fincher was in there. When Ken nodded Hernan' then said, "I was born in that house. My parents are buried out behind the goat corral." He looked at Ken and shrugged. "It's not right to kill a man in that house."

Ken stared. He'd learned from years in the Southwest that Mexicans as well as Indians had some solemn convictions. He'd come across Indians who would squat beside a dying person and the moment they heard the death rattle, they dragged them out of the hogan by the ankles so that they would not die in the house. If they died in there the Indians moved, built another hogan, and would never go near the old hogan.

Mexicans were less superstitious — some of them, anyway — but as he gazed at Hernan', the lined and graying *mayordomo*, he thought that Hernando's generation had their own set of rules.

He said, "We can set here all night until he gets thirsty enough to come out."

Hernan' returned his dark gaze to the jacal. "Did you try to talk him out?"

Ken rolled his eyes. "For the last half hour."

Hernan' continued to regard the square structure of adobe and stone. He hardly raised his voice when he said, "*Bastardo,* I have two sticks of dynamite in my saddlebags. And enough fuse."

He and Ken waited. It was a long wait but eventually Fincher answered, "You're bluffing."

Without another word Hernan' walked back to his horse and with his back to the jacal he said, "I want to see you die," and both Castleton and the rigid-faced man peeking around the corner of the front window saw his arms working as though unbuckling some saddlebags.

Fincher yelled at Ken. "Stop that crazy idiot!"

Ken neither looked toward the house nor replied.

When Hernan' faced them the bottom buttons of his shirt were open, there were two bulges holding the shirt partly away from his body. He was coiling something around his left hand, and he was smiling.

Fincher yelled again for Castleton to stop the *mayordomo,* and as before Ken did not even look around. Fincher swore and raised his six-gun to the rotten old wooden sill. Hernan' called a quick warning and both men fell to the ground as Fincher fired.

They drove him from the window with their combined return gunfire. Hernan' waited for the echoes to die, then hardly raised his voice as he said, "I give you ten seconds. Come out or I'll throw one stick through the window."

Ken held his breath. The sun was almost gone, their world this far south of the Miller yard was turning rusty red. Time did not appear to pass at all for a full minute, then Fincher flung his six-gun out the window, said he was coming out, and Ken saw the old door open a little as Fincher peeked out. "I ain't armed," he called. "Castleton, you watch the crazy Mexican."

"Come out," Ken replied. "I'l watch him."

Fincher appeared in the doorway, hung there long enough for someone to fire, and when no one did he stepped completely out of the building. His shirtfront was sticking to his body as he ignored Castleton and stared steadily at the dark, husky man lying beside Castleton with a gun in his fist.

Ken arose slowly, leathered his Colt, and bent down to beat off dust. Hernan' remained flat with his six-gun aimed at Pete Fincher, but his face was less rigid and his curled finger inside the trigger guard backed off a tad.

Ken went forward, picked up Fincher's gun, hurled it as far as he could, and jerked his

231

head for the rustler to walk toward Ken's horse. As the white-faced outlaw obeyed, he never once took his eyes off Hernan'.

The *mayordomo* arose, solemnly holstered his gun, and brushed himself off. He did not look at Pete Fincher, he looked at the spent horse dozing in tree shade. "It's a long way back," he said matter-of-factly. "You can't ride that horse, but you can lead him."

Ken told the outlaw to hold his arms straight out from his shoulders, pulled the man's shirt out, and yanked the money belt out. Each of its several little buttoned pockets was full but Ken did not look in them, he slung the belt over his shoulder and watched as Hernan' went to get the horse José had been riding when he'd been killed. He solemnly led him back and as he handed the reins to Fincher he asked an innocent question. "Are you hungry, *bastardo?*"

Fincher was indeed hungry but when he nodded his head he did it warily. The *mayordomo* fished inside his shirt and brought out a banana. Fincher neither took the banana nor said a word as both he and Ken stared at the *mayordomo*.

Hernan' explained in a quiet voice. "I put them in my saddlebags two days ago. I never liked to go for long without something to eat. Have this one, rider-of-other-people's-horses.

It is a little mushy but you can still eat it."
When Fincher made no move to take the banana Hernan' handed it to Ken, fished the
second one out of his shirt, considered its
shriveled, mottled appearance, and with a
shrug shoved it back inside his shirt.

CHAPTER 17

Clavenger

For the first mile nothing was said. Ken and Hernan' plodded along behind their captive and his exhausted horse.

The second mile Ken asked Pete Fincher who the man was who sneaked the weapons inside the jailhouse that had enabled the prisoners to escape.

Fincher was gnawing a corner of a plug and said nothing until he had his cud of molasses-cured tobacco pouched into his cheek. Then all he said was, "It don't matter."

They traversed another few yards when Hernan' drew his gun and cocked it. Up ahead, Fincher stiffened but kept on walking, and turned to look back. Hernan's gun was aimed at him and the vaquero was grinning.

"Answer," the *mayordomo* said.

Fincher answered, "It was the blacksmith's helper."

"Why would Mr. Clavenger's helper do that?" Ken asked, and got a surly reply.

"I knew him years back. Loaned him money to pay a fine and get out of jail. When I come here he was a lot more glad to see me than I was to see him. When he handed the guns through the bars he told me he was a feller who never failed to meet an obligation."

Hernan' put up his gun and slouched along eyeing Pete Fincher's back. Once, the attention of all three men was attracted by the sound of running horses. They halted, and as Ken stood in his stirrups, a band of about thirty *mesteños* raced southward with a few mares urging spindly-legged colts along.

Ken waited until they were lost to sight before sitting down and ordering Fincher to start walking.

He looked at Hernan'. "Something must have spooked them," he said and Hernan' shrugged. "They've always been down here. Since I was a child. The feed is good and they know every water hole. My father caught two of them one time. Do you know the saying that wild horses are too small for men and too mean for children? Well, my father finally was able to ride one of them but the other one — never. He turned that one loose." Hernan' smiled at the mustanger. "I could have told you where you built your trap you'd only catch Miller horses. Down here," Hernan' made a wild sweep with one arm.

"Down here you would have done better."

The sun failed, finally, night birds mourned from their secret places, and Pete Fincher's horse seemed to be recovering from his ordeal, at least he walked along with his head up, but the mounted men had no illusions; that animal had escaped being rendered useless by being windbroken by a very narrow margin. He would be usable again, but not for many months.

Ken opened two of the little pockets of the money belt. The light was too poor for him to count the money in each pocket, but he thumbed through, replaced the money, and slung the belt over his shoulder as Hernan' said, "How much?"

Ken did not know. For the present he had to take Fincher's word. "A lot," he said. "We'll count it when we get home."

Ken saw Fincher jettison his cud and asked if the outlaw was thirsty. Fincher answered over his shoulder, "Yes."

"It'll be another hour or two. Tell me something, Fincher. Where was that free grazer going with the Miller cattle?"

"Mexico."

Both Hernan' and Ken stared at the plodding man. "That'd be one hell of a long drive," Ken said.

Fincher shrugged. "It wasn't none of my

236

concern. What he did after he took 'em over an' I got my money didn't interest me. . . . But, like I told him, if I wasn't able to keep you'n Miz Miller's riders from picking up his trail, he was going to be in a peck of trouble."

"You tried," Hernan' said dryly.

Fincher did not reply. He was tiring. Like the men behind him he'd had enough adversity and excitement to wear any human being down, and now he was being taken back where there was a good chance he'd never reach Hermasillo and the jailhouse, he'd be lynched.

When they could make out distant pinpricks of light, he said, "Castleton, I'm a prisoner. It's up to you to keep folks away from me."

Hernan' laughed and although he said nothing he rode along for a short distance shaking his head.

They heard men talking up ahead in the still night. Castleton recognized one harsh voice and called out, "Clavenger!"

For ten seconds all noise up ahead subsided, then the harsh voice called back. "Castleton? We was goin' down to look for you, but it got too dark. You get Fincher?"

"Yeah. How's José?"

"Dead. Him and that half-breed friend of Fincher's."

They finally were able to make out the riders. It was a fairly large band of them. Pete Fincher stopped, stared, then turned to address Castleton. "Remember what I told you. I'm a prisoner. Keep 'em away from me."

Ken heard without heeding. He was trying to get an accurate count. Hernan' had already made it. "Nine," he said, "Counting the blacksmith."

Where the two groups came together with Pete Fincher between them, the riders from Hermasillo looked steadily at the outlaw over a period of silence. Will Clavenger had a white bandage that showed under his hat. He looked longest at Fincher, and dismounted as he said, "How come my helper snuck guns to you? You pay him?"

"Other way around," replied the outlaw. "He owed me one from a long way back."

Clavenger was set to speak again when Ken asked about Anna Marie, Betsy, her brother, and Gregorio. Clavenger tore his fierce stare away from Fincher long enough to answer. "Fine . . . considering. Some other fellers who come out with me took the half-breed an' the redheaded feller back to town."

"Sheriff Brown?"

The blacksmith returned his sulfurous glare to Fincher. "This son of a bitch shot him in his cell, like shootin' a rat in his cage."

Ken nodded to himself. So far everything

238

he had heard corroborated what Fincher had told them after leaving the jacal. Evidently Fincher knew it was too late to lie.

Ken lifted his rein hand. "Let's get back," he said, and a wiry, weathered man Ken recognized from having been with the earlier posse said, "Not so fast, mister."

The wiry man had a lasso rope looped loosely around his saddle horn. He was pulling off his roping gloves as he addressed the blacksmith. "Will? . . ."

Clavenger scowled at Ken and Hernando Iturbide. "We come down here for this son of a bitch or his carcass. You should have shot him when you had the chance. He's goin' to hang from the nearest tree."

Fincher stood beside his horse looking at Castleton. He'd been in trouble of one kind or another all his mature life. He had survived, but right now, with a sickly moon showing in a setting of brilliant stars, in the middle of nowhere, where nothing was familiar, he knew genuine fear. Castleton and the Mexican were facing nine men whose determination was plain even in the poor light.

"You're the law," Ken said to the burly blacksmith, and got a tart reply.

"That don't make any difference. Fincher's done just about everything bad in the book."

"So you'd let a bunch of townsmen hang him?"

Clavenger did not even hesitate. "Right here an' now, if we find a decent tree."

Ken glanced at the *mayordomo*. Hernan' was sitting his horse like a copper statue, looking at the men behind Clavenger.

The blacksmith ignored Hernan' and growled for Ken to dismount. Ken remained where he was. One of the town riders, a round-faced man with scanty hair with whom Castleton had talked after their earlier success, said, "Ain't no trees down here. A few spindly paloverdes that wouldn't hold up a man's weight. Back a mile or so there was some oaks."

Several of the other riders murmured agreement. But Ken had the feeling those men, for all their earlier ardor, were beginning to have second thoughts now that they had Fincher in front of them, and two stubborn armed men behind Fincher.

Lynching was a serious crime; even if the law did not touch them, they still had their individual consciences to consider. No one liked to look into his shaving mirror and see a murderer looking back. Particularly men from a town who had never seen a lynching before, let alone participated in one.

Ardor for vengeance, like anger, was not

240

something that could be maintained indefinitely, and these men who had been so furious and vengeful several hours earlier in town seemed to feel a lot less vengeful now in the cooling night.

The blacksmith dismounted and slowly walked ahead. He watched Hernan' particularly but when he spoke it was to Pete Fincher. "Why those two want to save your hide is beyond me, you murderin' son of a bitch."

Ken spoke quietly. "You can have Fincher, blacksmith, but we'll ride back to town with you."

The implication was not lost on any of the townsmen. One disgusted man said, "Take him up on it, Will. As far as I'm concerned this has been one damned fool thing after another. Take him up on it. As far as I'm concerned that lynchin' notion's gone sour. Let the law have the son of a bitch and let the law hang him proper."

There were several mutters of agreement. Pete Fincher, sweating like a stud horse, began to have a glimmer of hope. They still wanted to hang him, and maybe it would eventually happen, but Pete Fincher had been getting out of narrow squeaks like a greased pig for a long time. The more others procrastinated the more he dared hope and scheme.

Ken looked steadily at the blacksmith,

241

whose expression showed the man's inherent stubbornness. The townsmen made the decision for him.

"Okay," he exclaimed. "Let's get on with it."

The ride to Hermasillo was quiet. Some of the town riders felt sorry that the blacksmith had been made a fool of. Others were less charitable but kept it to themselves. Fincher rode in their midst as expressionless as a stone.

When they reached Hermasillo and rode down the middle of the main thoroughfare, people came out of shops and stores to stare in silence.

Clavenger rode the full distance to the jailhouse wearing a forbidding scowl. Some of the riders peeled off before the cavalcade got to the jail.

When the men dismounted and looped their reins at the jailhouse hitching post there were four of them and an embittered blacksmith. Ken, Gregorio, Hernan', and Chet.

When Pete Fincher was locked back into the same cell he had inhabited earlier Clavenger said, "I'll get a cell mate for you in a little while."

Fincher smiled bleakly. "Your helper? You damned fool, he left town when the rest of us busted out."

Clavenger seemed ready to launch himself

through the bars. Castleton nudged him toward the upper end of the narrow, dingy little corridor, and as he was doing this he faced the man in the cell. "Fincher, someday your mouth's goin' to get you killed."

The outlaw laughed.

Hernan' made coffee at the little potbellied stove. Gregorio went to stand in front of the racked-up weapons on the west wall, and while his back was to the others he asked a question.

"Where is the sheriff?"

No one knew. If Clavenger did he said nothing. He sat at the desk brooding.

Ken took coffee from the *mayordomo* but the blacksmith did not even look up, so Hernan' placed the cup atop the desk and filled two more cups, which nearly emptied the dented little speckleware pot.

It was uncomfortable in the office. Will Clavenger would look at none of them. He did not say a word even when they told him they had better head for home. As they were departing he put a venomous stare at the back of Hernando Iturbide, and a fresh flood of color filled as much of his face as was visible.

Ken and Hernan' stopped at the saloon after putting Fincher in jail.

Ken leaned on the bar. "Tell me something,

barman. Do you know a good man who can sort of wander down to the jail and set with the blacksmith?"

"At the jailhouse?"

"Yes."

"Why?"

"Well, he was mighty anxious to hang Fincher before we convinced him to bring the prisoner in. Now he's settin' in there like a brooding buzzard alone and Fincher's locked in his cell."

The burly man gazed steadily at Castleton for a moment before responding. "You think Clavenger might —"

"Mister, my guess is that he just might decide to strangle Fincher."

The barman said, "Not a bad idea. Save the price of a trial."

Castleton looked steadily back at the burly man. "Except that some of us rode our butts raw to make damned sure if Fincher hangs, it'll be accordin' to the law. Risked our necks to make sure. Now then, do you know anyone who could go down to the jailhouse?"

The barman made a wide sweep of his countertop with a sour rag before answering, and when he did answer he looked at Hernan'. "How about Carter Alvarado?"

Hernan' finished his jolt and blinked a couple of times before answering. "If he'd do it.

244

I haven't seen him in a long time. What's he doing now?"

"Riding gun guard for the stage company."

Ken asked Hernan' who Carter Alvarado was.

"He used to be a lawman in some border towns. He's not mean but folks got lots of respect for him."

Ken looked at the barman, who added a little more on the background of Carter Alvarado. "Nice feller, I've known him maybe six, eight years. Once or twice when Sheriff Brown run into more'n he could handle he'd deputize Carter. One time he cleaned out my saloon single-handed on a Saturday night."

"Is he around?"

The barman glanced in the direction of a wall clock and nodded. "He's about due over at the corral to go out with the afternoon stage. Hernan'? . . ."

The *mayordomo* nodded to Ken and left the saloon, heading for the corral.

"Carter's a good man. You'll like him," the barman said.

Ken did not have to like Carter Alvarado, he had no intention of being around Hermasillo any longer than he had to. All he wanted to be certain of was that what he and the others had gone through recently would not result in another jailhouse killing.

He asked the barman about Sheriff Brown. The burly man's reply was short. "He was buried yestiddy. A few folks went out to the cemetery, but not very many."

Ken asked about the blacksmith's helper who had smuggled the guns to the outlaws and the barman was equally brief. "He wasn't nowhere around. We looked high an' low but he left in a hurry, accordin' to the rooming house owner."

Hernan' returned with a man whose face was pock marked, and whose dark eyes were dead level when he spoke. Carter Alvarado was no more than average height, but muscular.

He shook hands with Castleton and nodded to the barman. Ken, Hernan', and the barman explained the situation at the jailhouse. Alvarado listened impassively.

Alvarado finally nodded. "Right now, today?" he asked, and when Ken nodded, the guard sighed. "They aren't goin' to like it over at the corral. There's a stage about ready to leave town. . . . Well, all right. I'll go tell them, then go down to the jailhouse. Clavenger won't like this."

CHAPTER 18

Castleton's Dilemma

Anna Marie was waiting when the men returned. She herded them into the kitchen and
fed them. Ken shoveled in food like there was
no bottom to his stomach.

That night as he lay in bed he thought about
a lot of things: the blacksmith, Hernan', and
how José had fallen off that horse as though
he'd been struck by a giant fist.

The next day Ken arose stiffly. He went
out to the washhouse to get cleaned up.

The bathhouse had been engineered by
someone who appreciated what was required.
Aside from a large zink tub, there was a stirrup
pump at the lower end that would fill the tub
from a well. The water was cold, but since
most of the bathing Castleton had done over
the past few years had been in creeks, cold
water troubled him a lot less than not bathing
at all.

There was one drawback: his filthy clothing.
He bathed slowly and thoroughly, lathered

heavily with the bar of brown lye soap kept in a dish nailed to the wall.

He dried off, pulled on a clean pair of britches and a clean but unironed shirt from his saddlebags, and shaved.

Anna Marie was standing on the porch. He closed the bathhouse door, saw her, and nodded. "Good morning, Miz Miller."

She showed no expression when she replied. "Good afternoon, Mr. Castleton."

He squinted at the location of the sun and shrugged.

"We'll be buryin' José in a little while," she said. "Mr. Castleton, have you considered that offer I made?"

He gazed at her. Damnedest thing; no matter how the lighting was, no matter what time of night or day he saw her, no matter even that her disposition was always chilly, though less so recently, she was a genuinely beautiful woman.

Not that Betsy wasn't; she was. But most young girls are just naturally pretty. Anna Marie Miller hadn't been young in a while. In fact, she had little pigeon wings of silver at the temples.

He pulled his thoughts back to her question. "I've been sort of busy lately," he told her. He started to walk away but changed his mind.

She spoke first. "You think I'm hard, and

I think you are stubborn."

"I'll admit I might be wrong about you, if you'll admit you might be wrong about me."

She looked at him. "But you *are* stubborn."

"Maybe, and maybe you think I'm stubborn because I'm having a hell of a time making up my mind."

"How long will that take? There are still the other cattle down south to be brought back. . . . That long?"

"About that long, maybe, ma'am."

She turned on him. "You know I don't like being called ma'am."

He hadn't actually been conscious of saying it so he apologized. "Slipped out. It's a habit I'll try to break. I'm sorry." He smiled and headed for the barn.

The sun was high, the air was clear and warm. The two vaqueros down in front of the barn were lifting a crude wooden box into a wagon that had a thick bed of hay in the bottom.

There were two bay horses on the tongue, with clean harness, and on each side of the seat someone had nailed a pair of coffee tins into which flowers had been placed.

Hernan' nodded without speaking and Gregorio did not even do that. He had been hit hardest by the death of José Elizondo. Anna Marie, Betsy, and Chet appeared on the

249

veranda across the yard, dressed properly for the burial, and Gregorio went deep into the barn to get their horses.

The little cavalcade left the yard slowly. The ranch cemetery was a mile west of the yard in a setting of old white oaks atop a slight roll of land. Someone, probably Frederick Miller, had kept livestock out through the erection of an elegant iron fence that someone else, probably a hired rider with considerable talent, had created in the shoeing shed.

The grave was open and waiting. Betsy was teary-eyed as they followed the old wagon.

Anna Marie was pale and expressionless. There were several graves out here. The one with a hand-chiseled granite block belonged to her husband.

Hernan' and Gregorio lowered the box with ropes. Hernan' kept a closed face, but Gregorio shed silent tears.

Anna Marie went to the edge and said a long prayer from memory. Ken watched her and marveled. He'd had trouble remembering the Lord's Prayer when as a child his mother had drilled him in it, and now he could not remember it at all.

When Hernan' and Gregorio began to fill the grave Ken went forward to help, the women returned to their horses. Chet searched the wagon for another shovel.

It was late afternoon before the wagon got back to the yard with Chet on horseback and the vaqueros with the wagon.

Later, Ken was out on the veranda for a smoke after supper. Anna Marie came out and softly said it was a beautiful night. He hadn't noticed but now he looked up. There were stars, but they seemed less distinct than on other nights, and although the moon was also up there, it too seemed to be slightly hazed over. He said, "Rain?"

She nodded as she took the chair beside him. "I think so. I hope so."

He waited a moment then mentioned her scattered cattle and she told him she thought she could bring back the main herd with the help of Betsy and Chet, Hernan', and Gregorio.

He looked at her. She was gazing down across the yard in the direction of the lighted bunkhouse. Perhaps sensing his look she turned and said, "I understand."

He scowled at her. "Understand what?"

"That you're not ready to settle down."

He looked away, shifted in the chair, and cleared his throat. This was not the Anna Marie Miller he had come to know, and this less imperious Anna Marie left him slightly uncomfortable.

She said, "Betsy is such a sweet girl."

251

He could have agreed with that, instead he remained silent.

"I suppose, in time, her brother will want to leave, too."

He had no answer for that.

"Could anyone convince him he'd be better off staying here where he'll have work as long as he wants it, and where he can . . . feel at home . . . like he belongs?"

Ken folded both hands in his lap with interlocking fingers. Anna Marie asking for advice increased his discomfort.

"Ken? . . ."

He deliberately watched the bunkhouse light before he replied. "You're asking the wrong man, Miz Miller. I haven't been his age in a long while."

"But once you were. You can remember, can't you?"

He shifted in the chair again. "I can remember, ma'am," he replied without realizing he had addressed her in the way she particularly did not like to be addressed. "I think that maybe if I'd had a place to settle in, a place like this with plenty to do and all, I most likely would have settled in."

"Could you talk to him? Ken, if he leaves, his sister will go with him. She's not ready yet. She's young and impressionable and . . ."

He understood what she had left unsaid. He'd been in towns where dancehall girls were as young as Betsy Conners.

"Yes'm, I can talk to him. I may not be very good at it, though."

"You'll be very good at it," she said, and watched his profile for a moment before speaking again. "Betsy, Chet, and I could probably round up the cattle and drive them back."

"With Hernan' and Gregorio," he told her.

"I had in mind sending them south to bring back the other band. If they're left down there too long they could find other cattle and join them. Getting them cut out again would take a long time, even if the stockmen down there helped."

He heaved a noisy sigh. She was making him feel guilty about leaving her when her cattle were scattered all over hell.

She sat watching him in the soft overhang gloom until he went to work rolling another smoke. When he lighted it she smiled at the resigned look.

"I'll help you," he said.

Her one mistake thus far was at this point. She should have left well enough alone, instead she said, "As a hired rider? I need three men, we've always had at the least that many permanent riders, and with the increase in calvy cows next spring . . ."

He killed the smoke and arose. "There'll be lots of time to think about that," he said, facing her. "Those cattle outside Thunder Valley'll have drifted with the feed by now. . . . When did you want to go after them?"

She also arose. "Tomorrow?"

He blinked. "It'll take tomorrow to shoe horses, load the wagon, and figure things out."

She softly smiled. "Day after tomorrow?"

When he nodded she said, "Good night. There's hot coffee on the stove," and went inside.

He leaned on the veranda railing. Since yesterday she had been different. He decided she needed him right now, so she had become more friendly, which wasn't exactly the word he would have used to describe this different Anna Marie Miller, but he could not find a better one.

He went to the kitchen, filled a cup with black java, and sat for a while at the kitchen table. The big old house was as silent as a tomb, with only an occasional creak and groan as the night turned chilly.

It was not helping bring her cattle back that bothered him, nor the prospect of an increased herd next spring. It was the association between them if he hired on. She would be his employer, he would be her hired hand. The vaqueros seemed to have no difficulty with that, but it was different for him.

CHAPTER 19

Beyond Thunder Valley

They did, indeed, have to reshoe horses, including the dinner-plate-sized hooves of the team of bays who had not worn shoes since the previous summer.

Ken put Chet to work removing wagon wheels whose burrs were threaded counterclockwise so that turning wheels tightened rather than loosened the wheels.

Chet slathered axle grease as thick as cold molasses on each hob and axle. He also replaced leather grease retainers, something Gregorio showed him how to do as he was passing. It was not a difficult job but since each wheel had to be hoisted by a ratchet jack, it was a time-consuming chore.

Hernan' and Ken finished shoeing the bay team and brought the using horses from the corral to the shoeing shed, by which time the sun was almost directly overhead.

By late afternoon they finished shoeing, had the wagon ready, and Anna Marie helped them load the supplies; at least, she told them what to load.

Shortly before sundown the vaqueros had only to roll their bedding, take whatever personal possessions their needs would require, and pile bedrolls and waterbags in the wagon.

By sundown the yard was quiet, the corralled horses had been turned out, and a lazy spindrift of smoke arose above the bunkhouse.

At dusk Ken and Chet went to the trough to wash up. Afterwards, they sat in the warm evening talking. It was an excellent opportunity for Ken to mention what was troubling Anna Marie.

After a lengthy preamble concerning his own wanderings and what little genuine satisfaction he had derived from them, he said, "You're young. The world beckons. Maybe South Pass most of all. If it was just you, I'd say go ahead, cover a lot of ground and meet folks, but it's not just you, is it?"

Chet was buttoning his shirt when he replied. "Someday she'll get married."

Ken nodded. "Someday."

The younger man perched on the edge of the trough. "She likes it here. More than any other place we been. She told me that. She thinks the sun rises and sets in Miz Miller's smile."

Ken said, "Uh-huh," without looking at

Chet and said what had been obvious over time. "Miz Miller thinks the world of your sister."

The youth nodded and Ken gazed in the direction of the main house where lamps had been lighted although it was not dark. "She never had any kids," he said musingly and more to himself than to the youth. The rest of that thought he kept to himself, but a woman Anna Marie's age most likely should have had children.

This was another area where his opinion arose from intuition and he was not comfortable thinking like that, so he also said, "Someday, in some far-off line shack maybe up in Wyoming or Montana, you'd think back. The hell of it is, Chet, by then you'll be too old to go back. . . . I know what I'm talkin' about."

Chet eyed the mustanger with curiosity. "That's the way it was with you?"

"Well, yes. In a different way, but yes. The trail goin' out is fresh and pleasant, but the trail back just don't exist."

The youth yanked Ken out of his reverie with a question. "But you're goin' to go on, aren't you? Betsy said Miz Miller offered you a full-time job and you told her you wasn't ready to settle in just yet."

Ken felt heat in his face and fell to minutely

examining the toes of his scuffed old boots. Anna Marie had to have told that to Betsy; the girl hadn't been on the veranda when he'd said it. Damn women, anyway!

A sudden thought occurred to him. Anna Marie needed someone to talk to, to confide in. It must have been hell on her having to act like a man in running the FM outfit.

This thought softened his resentment a little. He said, "Well, maybe, Chet. And maybe I've found what I've been waiting to find and am too dumb to know it."

"You'll stay on, then?"

Ken squinted in the poor light at his boots. Somewhere during his attempt to act like the father he had never been, and had no experience at trying to be, this damned palaver had got out of hand.

Chet watched Ken stand up, and said, "If you stay, I'll stay. Maybe it's like you said, a man gets to drifting, he won't be able to go back."

Ken faintly frowned in the gathering night. "Look around, Chet. What you see is a big cow outfit that'll only get better as time goes on. A man with a lick of sense would see this and want to be a part of it — settle in and have somethin' to work for."

The youth was silent for a long time. He only spoke again as Ken turned to leave the barn area. "You stay, Mr. Castleton, an' I'll stay."

Ken glared in the direction of the lighted main house before going to the bunkhouse to turn in.

The vaqueros were playing pedro at the battered old table where they ate, did their sewing, and just about everything else that required a flat surface. They looked up, looked longest at Castleton, and Gregorio went after the big old dented coffeepot.

Gregorio said, "If we are to roll out before sunrise, we had better down the coffee and go to bed."

Ken lay on his back in the darkness watching a distant star through the front window. He had no recollection when he fell asleep, but the smell of coffee awakened him and Gregorio's smile made him shove up out of his bunk with a grimace. He had all his life been an early riser, usually before men he had known who'd had consciences that did not permit them to sleep long, rolled out.

They ate a filling breakfast of tortillas and meat fried until it had curled like ancient leather, washed down with coffee strong enough to float a horseshoe, and went out into a chilly predawn with only heaven-sent light to brighten their progress in the direction of the corrals and the barn.

They were bundled against the cold and said very little, but went about the harnessing and the saddling, leaving the animals standing while they made certain they had forgotten nothing and were ready to ride when Anna Marie and Betsy arrived to say good-bye. Ken and Anna Marie Miller looked steadily at each other until the *mayordomo* led his horse out front to be mounted, then Ken and Chet did the same.

It was morning but looked no different than it had at midnight. Gregorio tooled the wagon with one hand, rolled his first cigarillo of the day with his free hand, lighted up and settled back, an epitome of a man comfortable in an environment and of which he knew no other.

The wagon rattled but its wheels turned without a sound from the hubs. Horses lustily blew their noses, a startled band of cattle fled so fast they showed only a momentary flash of white rear ends, and although the sun was crouching below the eastern curve of the world, it would not spring forth to birth a new day for several more hours.

Hernan' rode beside the wagon when he thought Gregorio should alter course slightly so as to minimize the distance to be covered. Gregorio leaned down, spat out his smoke, stamped it to death against the floorboards, and ignored the *mayordomo*'s instruction for

261

a full mile, then began a long, slow north-westerly curve. He did not look at the *mayordomo* and Hernan' did not look at him, but as Hernan' rode ahead he rolled his eyes and sighed.

When the sun arrived, filling the world with morning brilliance as fast as the speed of light, the FM crew was within sight of those westerly ridges where the trail led through to another huge expanse of grassland on the other side.

Hernan' did as he usually did in these circumstances, he loped ahead. He took his scouting responsibility very seriously.

Soon Hernan' rode back. He had not gone very far up into the pass to the next expanse of open country, just far enough to hear cattle lowing as they stirred out of their sleep.

He said he did not think they were as scattered as he had feared. Castleton kept his own counsel. Cattle drifted; give them a thirst and they would drift.

Ken asked Hernan' where the nearest water was and the *mayordomo* understood perfectly what was in Castleton's mind. He made a wide gesture northward. "Three miles. A creek." As he lowered his arm he smiled at the mustanger. "Some are ahead on the far side, but the others will be up there. They may drift back down here after they drink, *quién sabe?*"

They left Gregorio with the wagon, went up the trail to the top with the sun at their backs. As yet it had very little warmth in it.

From the top the *mayordomo* was proven correct. The FM cattle visible to the west were mostly wet cows with spindly-legged calves who had probably already been north to tank up before their calves were stirring.

They started down the slope. The cattle did not notice riders until they were well along on the flat country in their direction, then they got between their calves and the horsemen, heads high, still as statues.

They found the cattle as the *mayordomo* had predicted, grazing peacefully along the moist bank of a creek that was partially lined with willows, though their screening effect was insufficient to keep the water cold as it traversed miles of open countryside.

Hernan' and Ken dismounted up there, slipped their bridles to water their horses, and watched the nearest cattle, who were beginning to edge farther from the riders.

Ken said, "They look good, Hernan'. I don't mean just in good flesh. They look up-bred."

The *mayordomo* watched the cattle almost with fondness. "The *patrón* came here with stock from Texas. He brought in good bulls. Mostly, they didn't last long. They came from soft ground and green grass. First, they got sore-footed, then they suffered during long dry spells. But he would bring in more until, like you can see, FM has the best upgraded beef anywhere around."

Ken gazed at the lined, weathered dark face. "What was he like, Hernan'?"

"An honest man who worked hard and expected others to do the same. If they didn't . . ." Hernan' shrugged. "He chased away the Indians. He hanged horse or cattle thieves wherever we caught them."

"A hard man, Hernan'?"

The vaquero was torn between loyalty and the truth, but eventually he nodded. "*Sí*. If a rider did his work, they got along. If he was a little slack, they didn't get along."

"How long did you work for him before he died?"

Hernan' puckered his eyes in the direction of the cattle before answering. "Ten years, maybe twelve, it makes no difference, does it?"

Ken shook his head. "No difference. Does his widow pull her weight?"

This time when the *mayordomo* smiled, it was a kind of soft, perhaps fatherly smile. "She had to learn a lot of things fast. I knew this was so. She never rode with us before. She was different then. She did not smile often.

She worked late. I saw the lamp burning many nights very late. . . . She changed, *amigo.* Before, she was very pretty and — maybe more like a lady."

"She's still a lady, Hernan'."

"Yes. But in a different way. She had to change a lot. FM is a large ranch with many cattle and horses and sometimes not enough rain." The *mayordomo* shrugged and stepped ahead to rebridle his horse. He said no more as the two of them began a wide surround without haste, gradually bringing hundreds of cattle together on the south side of the creek.

Two men could not drive that many cattle without a lot of loss, especially when they passed dense thickets of brush where savvy, sly older cows could fade from sight in a twinkling, but they did not really attempt to drive them as much as they bunched them and let a few leaders take a southward route.

When Chet and Gregorio came up, they also got behind the cattle, down both sides, and kept them moving back toward Thunder Valley.

CHAPTER 20

Something to Remember

Chet had jerky in a saddlebag. Ken hunted up twigs for a warming fire, shared the jerky, and afterward rolled a smoke. Chet watched, and when Castleton lighted up the youth inhaled deeply of fragrant smoke, but when Ken offered him the makings, he declined with a candid explanation.

"I tried it a few times an' got sick, but I like the smell. It's sort of like coffee cooking, it never tastes as good as it smells."

Ken smiled and poked the fire until sparks flew. Around them in the night, cattle lowed. The next morning they pushed the cattle a little farther from the pass through the timbered uplands, then headed for the home place. Gregorio surprised everyone but Hernan' when he knocked a harmonica on his knee and, with the lines slack, played a Mexican song.

He surprised them because of his talented rendition; cattle country was full of men who played mouth harps, but extremely few played well.

The sun reddened behind clouds as it sank closer to the rims. A storm was on the way.

They ambled part of the way back, watching the heavens over their shoulders. Those ominous black clouds had stealthily come over the northeasterly rims and were spreading rapidly. The riders were as yet on the fringe of the storm, but a chilly wind that gusted around them a mile from the yard scattered their last doubts that a real gully washer was on the way.

Gregorio bounced along behind the riders. Occasionally he looked over his shoulder. The impression he got was that the storm was pursuing them, not rapidly but relentlessly. He whistled at the bays again.

The mustanger had a tightly rolled old slicker behind his saddle, which he freed from its bindings with reins around his horn to free both hands.

By the time they reached the yard the slicker was wet-shiny. Anna Marie and Betsy came out to help them, even though they too were soon thoroughly wet.

The women ran for the house to light the stove while the men were busy offsaddling.

Ken stood in the doorway watching Anna Marie run for the house.

The storm that had been nibbling around the yard abruptly seemed to empty its dark clouds with rain falling so rapidly it had no time to soak into the parched ground.

What brought Ken and Chet straight up was the first roll of thunder. It sounded as though it had originated in the yard. Gregorio was already over at the bunkhouse shoving kindling into the little iron stove, but Hernan' walked over to Ken and said, "It will get louder."

As he pulled down his hat, pushed up his shoulders, and followed Gregorio's example by racing for the bunkhouse, another of those thundrous explosions came, as Hernan' had predicted, louder than the earlier one.

Water fell in sheets. Ken and Chet stood in the barn door watching as the rain did not come straight down, it came in solid ranks, one after the other. Water ran everywhere in rivulets.

Chet was saying he thought they had better make a dash for the bunkhouse when there was a peal of thunder that actually made the barn shake.

Ken shared with the younger man an instinctive feel of total disaster, like the end of the world. He had been through dozens of storms, but never before one whose thunder made the ground quiver.

They made a run for it, got inside as another explosion of thunder arrived, this time causing the lighted lamp to vibrate on its overhead wire.

Gregorio was making coffee and dripping water where he stood. Hernan' had his back to the little stove. He grinned.

Ken had a moment to tell Chet he now understood why it was called Thunder Valley. In that same moment Hernan' said, "The Indians would not stay here. They would hunt in the valley but they had some belief that the Great Evil Spirit lived here. The thunder was his roar of anger."

Ken had no time to comment, another of those incredibly loud crashes shook the bunkhouse and the ground beneath it.

Ken peeked out the door, across the little porch in the direction of the main house. Smoke was trying to rise from the chimney and the kitchen stovepipe, but water was beating it back as soon as it was clear of the roof.

He went to stand with Chet and Hernan' by the stove, where clothing, redolent of horse sweat, steamed, as Gregorio put three cups of steaming black coffee on the table and went back to fill one for himself.

To Gregorio and Hernan', the unnerving deafening sounds appeared natural, except that they interrupted their attempts at conversation.

When there was no thunder the noise of rain on the bunkhouse roof made it necessary to yell to be heard, so there was very little conversation.

The men drank coffee, dried out by the stove, and waited. When the storm did not appear to be letting up Hernan' broke out the bunkhouse's greasy deck of cards and everyone sat down to play pedro.

Eventually Gregorio prepared a meal, and no one could have complained if they had wanted to. Between the incessant pounding on the roof and the deafening intermittent thunder, it was almost impossible to speak or be heard.

When there was a slight lull Ken asked Hernan' how long these storms lasted, and both vaqueros smiled. "Sometimes only overnight, sometimes two or three days."

Another peal made the overhead lamp sway violently again.

CHAPTER 21

An Additional Unpleasantness

The storm lasted all night. The next day sunlight did not break through the clouds until late the following afternoon.

The yard was a series of runnels and heavy mud. Little could be done and little was done, only the chores and meals and more pedro, but by evening, with the runoff diminishing and restlessness setting in, Ken crossed to the porch of the main house and knocked. Anna Marie looked up at him. "Did I tell you how the ranch got its name?" she asked, and he nodded, not sure whether she had or not.

"The ground'll be hard enough tomorrow. Hernan', Chet, Gregorio, and I'll go south for the other cattle," he said.

She gazed steadily at him for a long time. No one had spoken to her as though they were stating a fact in a long time.

She stepped out onto the porch and closed

the door after herself, but by the time she had done these things and was facing him again, the annoyance was gone.

She was going to say she would accompany them when she remembered the last time she had said that, and what his reaction had been. She looked out over the soggy yard and back. "It might be better to wait another day," she told him. "If the sun stays out the ground will dry fast."

His reply suggested that he just might be as stubborn as she had said. "We don't have to make any kind of time. It won't be hard on the horses."

Her annoyance returned, but atrophied faster this time. "All right. If the cattle have mixed with local ones down there —"

"I'll take care of that," he said, and smiled. "We should be back in two or three days. . . . I'll be hungry as a wolf."

She did not return his smile. The process of getting accustomed to each other seemed to depend upon her ability, and willingness, to agree with him. As she turned toward the door, she said, "Good luck."

He stopped her dead in her tracks. "Anna Marie?"

She turned. He had never before used her given name although she had called him by his.

He seemed as shocked as she was, but in fact what he had intended to say seemed so unwarranted that he groped for something to replace it with.

"We'll take our time," he stated lamely. "No need to sweat any more tallow off the cattle."

She remained facing him for a long moment before nodding. "Of course," she replied, and went back into the house.

When Betsy came to the parlor Anna Marie was standing with her back to the door. Betsy asked if she felt all right and Anna Marie smiled and nodded, then went to the kitchen, the refuge of most women when they needed a little quiet time.

The sun shone briefly that afternoon, steam rose from the yard, and Gregorio went to the woodpile out back to replenish the boxful no one had been able to refill during the storm.

Ken mentioned heading south in the morning as the riders were eating supper. They were willing; boredom had also made them restless.

The sky would be clear in the morning and as the day advanced the ground would become firm. There was no need to depart at dawn as was customary, they could not hurry in any event, nor did it matter greatly when they got back. It only mattered that they brought back a hundred head of Anna Marie's cattle.

Habits die hard. Ken rolled out just ahead of sunrise and went down to the barn to pitch feed and give each using horse a half can of rolled barley. They would not be ridden hard today, but they had been ridden fairly hard the previous days.

Gregorio had breakfast ready, beef cooked until it could have been used to resole boots, but at least his fried potatoes were golden brown and his coffee, a little strong, was no less than his diners were accustomed to.

The two vaqueros and Ken ate while Chet was over at the main house saying good-bye to his sister.

They were down at the barn getting ready to ride when Chet appeared, accompanied by Anna Marie. This time she took Ken aside without regard of what the others thought, and told him bluntly to be careful. When he asked why, she told him her husband had once had a run-in down there with a cowman named Douglas. She did not say whether that was the man's first or last name.

It was his last name. His first name was Angus.

Ken smiled about her warning. "The cattle are marked. Whoever Douglas is or whatever he thinks, FM isn't a brand a man could overlook. We'll be careful." He reached for her hand with the vaqueros surreptitiously watching and squeezed it. For a second she did not respond, then she squeezed back.

Later, as they were riding out of the yard, Anna Marie watched them go and waved. They all waved back, but excepting Chet Conners, the riders knew her wave was meant for Ken.

They were halfway to Hermasillo when Hernan' looked back, thought he saw a rider in the distance, shrugged, and faced forward.

It was a beautiful day with an azure sky overhead and spongy earth underfoot. The larks were back, as were other birds who sought bugs in the grass. A ground owl who had either returned to his burrow late, or who belatedly detected the sounds of horsemen passing, poked his piquant little face out and watched.

They loped for a while. The gravelly ground south and east of Hermasillo was quicker to dry out on top.

A little cold breeze coming off a snowpack somewhere ruffled the grass and splayed horses' tails, but passed along before the riders freed their jackets and put them on.

They made better time than they had made on their previous southward ride. They chewed jerky, enjoyed the warmth, the glass-clear air that made visibility perfect, and once when they halted at a creek to tank up their animals and Hernan' said it was like a pleasure ride, Ken gave him a sardonic look.

They headed more easterly when they had the crumbly ridges that encircled the abandoned ranch in sight, picked up their earlier tracks and followed them until they topped out with a view of the old ranch and most of its surrounding countryside.

There was dust in the yard below and westerly. Men were down there, some on horseback, some on foot.

Gregorio made an indignant curse. "They have a branding fire."

Evidently they'd been working their fire for several hours. The men atop the eastern ridge sat motionless for a long while, until they were satisfied with what they saw, then started down the same loose-rock trail they had traversed earlier, paying little attention to the footing of their animals as they watched a cow roped fore and aft as a sweating man ran to her with a hot iron.

The cow bawled, rolled her eyes, and with her tongue protruding, fought to retain her upright stance until the ropers rode out a ways, then she toppled onto her side.

Hernan' swore fiercely in two languages and yanked loose the tie-down holding his six-gun in its holster. Behind him Gregorio and Chet did the same. Only Ken Castleton rode without freeing his gun. He had singled out the head man down there. He was a thick, gray individual standing next to a thousand-pound gray horse. Neither he nor the four other men with him saw strangers approaching until the man with the hot iron happened to glance up before applying the brand.

He stepped back holding the iron in both gloved hands, and the graying man bellowed at him because branding irons cooled rapidly.

The man with the iron pointed with it and all the other men turned to watch as Ken, Chet, and two vaqueros rode at a dead walk straight toward them.

The thick, gray man said, "Son of a bitch!" and when a nearby rangeman asked if he knew the strangers he answered sharply. "Not them two out front, but them Messicans ride for FM."

He did not have to explain; his hired hands had been rebranding FM cattle all morning.

One of the older man's riders straightened around very slowly, ran a gloved hand under his nose, and said, "Well, you got the bill of sale, Mr. Douglas," and a lanky, weathered man snorted. He was standing to one side of the man named Douglas, and the rider who had mentioned a bill of sale began to frown at the older man, but he said no more.

Hernan' came up first, halted, placed both gloved hands atop the saddle horn, and looked from the struggling cow to the riders holding her with their dallies, from them to the burly, gray man, and to the darkly weathered, lanky man nearby.

Ken loosened in the saddle, studied the scene around him, and nodded pleasantly at the burly man. "You'll be Douglas?" he asked, and got back a short reply.

"I'm Angus Douglas. Who are you?"

"Name's Castleton. This lad's name is Chet Conners."

Angus Douglas scowled. "All right. I've seen them other two. What d'you want?"

"A hundred head of FM cattle some rustlers drove down here an' left. Like that cow you got stretched out to mark."

The boyish cowhand who had mentioned the bill of sale earlier spat aside before he said, "You work for FM?"

Hernan' nodded.

"My uncle's got a bill of sale for these cattle."

Ken smiled at the youth who was about Chet's age, maybe a tad younger. "I'd like to see it," Ken said.

The youth turned toward the burly gray man. "Show it to 'em. We're wastin' time."

The man fished inside his shirt pocket, drew forth a limp, crumpled scrap of paper, and held it out.

Ken eased ahead until he was close enough, sat a long moment gazing at the paper held out, then turned toward Hernan'. "Signature's even worse this time," he said, as he lazily tugged loose the tie down over his six-gun and turned back toward the older man. "If you didn't write that, Mr. Douglas, who did?"

The leathery individual hooked both thumbs in his cartridge belt and glared. "What kind of a damned question is that?" he demanded. "You boys come here for trouble, you're likely to get a bellyful."

The youth standing a slight distance from his uncle began tugging off his gloves. His cartridge belt and Colt were hanging from the brake handle of an old wagon near the barn. For the kind of work he and the other men on foot had been doing, a weighty belt and weapon provided nothing but interference.

The heavyset older man did not blink in his regard of Ken Castleton. He shoved the paper back into a shirt pocket by feel and did not speak until the paper was pocketed. Then he said, "Are you accusin' me of forgin' a bill of sale, mister?"

Ken continued to smile a little. "No. Not if that's not what you did. But that's not Anna Marie Miller's signature, Mr. Douglas."

The man faced Hernando Iturbide. "Who the hell does he think he is?"

Hernan', boiling inside at what was obviously misbranding, answered coldly. "He rides with us. Him and the feller beside him. If he says that's not the *señora*'s signature, then it is not." Hernan' leaned on his saddle horn. "I think to make it legal, you can give us a bill of sale for the cattle you have misbranded and we'll round them up and start for home."

The men on the ground were silent as they looked at Angus Douglas. They, too, had left their weapons at the wagon. Only Douglas and the weathered, lanky man near him were armed.

It was the lanky man who spoke next. "Tell you what," he said. "Turn them horses around and ride back the way you come."

Ken, Chet, and the vaqueros centered their attention on this man. Hernan' was angry all the way through. He said, "Give us the bill of sale for the rebranded FM cattle, and get away from here, and we'll do the rest."

The lanky man stepped up closer to Angus Douglas. Whether he was a good stockman or not, he most certainly was not an individual who wore a gun without being experienced in its use.

He was going to reply to Hernan' when the burly man brushed his arm with his fingers. Angus Douglas had lived long enough to realize that when trouble came, he and the lanky man facing five armed and hostile riders had about as much chance of surviving a gunfight as a crippled saint being pursued by the devil. He, too, was about to speak when the youth who had first challenged the FM riders raised an arm as he said, "Riders."

He was correct. It seemed to be five of them approaching from the direction of the westerly stage road. Only the lanky man did not look, he was watching Hernan' and Ken Castleton.

The men working the branding fire watched for a moment, then walked over to the old wagon for their weapons.

Ken drew, cocked his six-gun, and called to them. "Hold it right where you are!"

They stopped short of the wagon as the oncoming horsemen hooked their mounts into a fast gait and did not slack off until they were at the edge of the yard.

In front was the interim sheriff, Carter Alvarado. Behind him were four men whose full attention was on the drama in the yard.

Angus Douglas blustered, showed Alvarado his bill of sale, and Hernan' called in Spanish that it was a forgery. Alvarado leaned down, took the paper, pocketed it, and said, "Drop your gun," to the burly man. When he hesitated, and while the leathery man's attention was briefly diverted, Hernan' drew his six-gun and cocked it. The lanky man turned very slowly. Gregorio had also fisted his Colt. Ken offered the lanky man some good advice. "Get rid of the gun, mister."

The weathered man very slowly lifted out his weapon and let it fall.

Sheriff Alvarado rode among the cattle, sat his horse longest where the man with the cooling iron was standing beside the downed cow, and reached for the iron, which the cowboy handed to him. Alvarado rode over to Angus Douglas, tossed the iron at his feet and said, "If you give them a bill of sale for the misbranded cattle, that'll end it." Alvarado fished the bill of sale from his pocket and handed it to Angus Douglas. "Write it on the back," he said, and offered a stub of a pencil, then Alvarado and the others waited.

• Angus Douglas moved toward the lanky man, told him to stand still, and used the man's back to write out the bill of sale transforming title of all FM cattle that had been rebranded with his own mark to Anna Marie Miller.

He went over, handed the paper to Sheriff Alvarado, who read it while sitting loose in his saddle, pocketed it, and said, "Now get your traps in the wagon, mount up your men, and get the hell away from here. . . . And, Mr. Douglas, if I ever have to come after you again. . . . I'll bury you." Alvarado raised

282

dark eyes to the lanky man. "What's your name?"

"Hank Billingsly."

Alvarado acknowledged that with a curt nod, gazed steadily at Billingsly for a moment, then returned his attention to Angus Douglas. "I said load up and leave. Do it!"

It required half an hour for Douglas and his men to load up, get astride, and head west in the direction of the stage road. Not until they were well beyond gun range did the sheriff finally dismount. He shook his head at Hernan'. "We'll help you make the gather and head back. We're down here anyway."

It took most of the early afternoon to make a head count and line the cattle out in a northwesterly direction, the only route available that did not involve climbing treacherous upland footing again.

Hernan' and Alvarado rode in the drag where the sheriff told Hernan' something that really surprised him.

"I had to leave town yesterday. While I was gone they took Fincher down to the livery barn and hanged him from a barn balk."

Hernan' stared and Carter Alvarado wagged a finger at him. "That's all I know, so don't ask questions. They will bury him beside Sheriff Brown today. This morning, in fact, so it will be done by the time we get back."

They looked steadily at one another for a moment and afterwards Hernan' accepted Carter Alvarado's admonition, he asked no questions.

CHAPTER 22

"... For a While"

They had the lights of Hermasillo on their right and ahead when full dark settled, but they were still a fair distance from town. The cattle were tired, they would not spread much until dawn, but Ken said he and Chet would remain with them. Sheriff Alvarado did not care what disposition was made, he had completed what he had set out to do and was willing to leave other things to the FM men.

Hernan' and Gregorio rode away with Carter Alvarado. What had interested Hernan' ever since the town riders had entered the yard of the old ranch was how Alvarado had happened along.

The answer was simple. "The lady came to me," he told Hernan'. "She told me what was going forward." Alvarado shrugged. "I found four men and went down there. The lady was right."

Hernan' squinted in the direction of town lights. "It was a good time when you arrived," he said, and all three of them laughed, but just before entering Hermasillo the *mayordomo* remembered something: that distant rider he had seen behind them in the early morning.

Ken and Chet Conners divided most of their time, at least for several hours, taking turns nighthawking, but the cattle were weary, they were content to bed down, hunger could wait until sunup for both cattle and men. The cattle had grazed along and the men had jerky, it was the riding stock that spent most of the night hopping with their hobbles from one mouthful to the next.

Ken and the lad talked for a while, but they, too, needed sleep. Fortunately it was a mild night. Not all nights this time of year were compatible to men who slept on the ground under one or two blankets.

But that depended a lot on how tired men were.

Ken awakened feeling chilly, rolled out in the dark to coax a little fire to life and warm himself. Northward there were no more than three or four lights showing in Hermasillo. He heard the cattle but would not be able to see them for another hour or so.

When Chet awakened, pulled on his boots, and went out to see where the horses were, Ken felt his face. It was again rough and stubbly. As Chet was returning two riders appeared bundled against the chill. Hernan' had rousted the café man out and under his disagreeable glare had made the man bring enough food for hungry men after he and Gregorio had eaten their fill.

During their meal Hernan' told Ken and Chet who it was that had sent Carter Alvarado to the old ranch. Chet seemed pleased but Ken ate in silence for a long while, and only when there was enough pink in the sky for the roundup to be undertaken did he tell Hernan' that while he appreciated Anna Marie's concern, he did not like it, that the five of them could have handled whatever erupted down in the yard of the old ranch.

Hernan' veered after some cows who were already grazing away from where they should be, and rolled his eyes. He told his horse that if the *señora* and the mustanger would just try a little harder to be frank with one another it would be helpful to what, he told the uninterested horse, Hernan' was convinced was going to eventually be a good relationship. He stopped just short of confiding in the horse he had seen enough signs over the past few weeks to know what had started out as mutual dislike had, with the passage of time, become something else.

The sun arrived. One moment it was gray,

the next moment it was light, but as always, there would be little warmth in the rising sun until it got well above the horizon.

They angled the cattle in the direction of FM grass, which took them well west of Hermasillo.

They were well on their way when the interim sheriff rode out to reassure himself. Ken said he appreciated what Alvarado had done, and by way of acknowledgment got a shrug meaning *por nada*. As the Mexicans said, it was only what people did for one another and required no thanks.

Alvarado saw Hernan' loping back to where he and Ken were riding. He anticipated what a three-way conversation would involve and was ready when Hernan' greeted him, then asked about Pete Fincher.

"I told you yesterday," the sheriff replied. "I had to be out of town for part of the day. The liveryman said someone had stolen horses from his fenced pasture against the foothills."

"And had they?" Hernan' asked.

"No. The fence was down. The horses just stepped over the wire and walked away. . . . No, Hernan', I did not bring them back. I told the liveryman where they were and he went out to put them back and fix the fence."

Hernan' cleared his throat and Carter Alvarado did as he had done once before, he raised a hand and wagged a finger. "I don't know any more than I told you yesterday. They took Fincher down to the livery barn and left him hanging from a big timber down there."

Ken saw that this explanation did not satisfy the *mayordomo* and spoke quickly, before Hernan' could.

"It's done, Sheriff. I tried to prevent it, but it's done and over with."

Alvarado nodded and smiled at Ken. He refused to look at Hernan'.

After Alvarado had struck out on the return ride to Hermasillo, Hernan' said, "Someday he will tell me the rest of it."

Ken gave him a puzzled look. "What more is there to tell? When he got called out of town they took Fincher out and lynched him. We did our damnedest to save him for a trial, but right now, Hernan', I'm willing to forget the whole damned mess. Fincher got what was coming to him. Not in the way I thought he ought to get it, but when you think about it, the end would have been the same no matter who did it."

Hernan' was squinting ahead where Chet Conners was edging a slight easterly drift back in the right direction. "Would you like to know what I think?" he asked.

Ken was straining to see rooftops and shaggy old trees and answered almost indifferently. "Sure. What do you think, *compañero?*"

"You don't know the liveryman, but I do. I think the liveryman went out, knocked down his own fence, and rode back to tell Carter someone had stolen his horses, and when Carter went out there, the liveryman and others who wanted Fincher dead lynched him."

Ken saw the older man turn slightly wearing a small, vague smile. "You care to know what else I think?"

Ken shrugged.

"I think Alvarado knew they were going to lynch Fincher."

"How, if they were careful?"

"Because, *compañero,* Carter Alvarado is no fool. Also because when he told me last night on the drive toward Hermasillo what had happened, he did as you saw him do this morning, he shook his finger at me and told me he had nothing more to say about it."

"Hernan', maybe he didn't have."

The *mayordomo,* who had known Carter Alvarado many years, laughed, gave Ken a sly, sidelong look, and went loping out where Chet was slouching along with warm sunlight on his back.

They used up most of the day driving the cattle past the Miller yard in a northwesterly direction, and left them up there where they could find the other cattle by scent.

It was late evening by the time they reached the yard, cared for their horses, and trooped over to the bunkhouse. There were two lights burning in the main house. Chet left the others at the bunkhouse porch and walked toward those two lights.

Hernan', Ken, and Gregorio removed their spurs, tossed their hats aside, took turns at the wash tub out back, and when the little iron stove had been fired up, they shared a solemn drink of whiskey from Gregorio's hidden bottle before supper was begun and full relaxation was possible.

Night settled quickly, tired men with full stomachs were having their final coffee and smoke of the day, each feeling satisfied with how things had turned out, except for the loss of José, when Chet walked in to say that Anna Marie wanted to see the mustanger.

Hernan' and Gregorio sipped coffee watching Ken. After he thanked young Conners for bringing the summons, he went to perch on the edge of a bunk, pull off his boots, hang his hat beside the bunk, and stood up to shed the cartridge belt and holstered weapon, then lay back and rolled onto his side. The vaqueros exchanged a wide smile.

Tonight no one was enthusiastic about cards

and the last one to bed down blew out the lamp, which brought immediate darkness to the bunkhouse.

Across the yard on the porch Anna Marie saw the light wink out and waited. Betsy came out to sit with her. She had a shawl around her shoulders. It was not chilly but it would be if they sat out there very long.

Distantly, cattle were lowing, otherwise the night was still and quiet. When Anna Marie said, "He's not coming," Betsy made a reasonable excuse. "They've been in the saddle a lot lately. My brother is the youngest and he told me he could sleep the clock around."

Anna Marie had nothing to say in reply. She sat a long while before eventually giving up and going inside where it was warmer. Betsy followed her.

When they said good night and parted Anna Marie did not face the girl; she went down the hall to her room and Betsy heard the door close.

For close to three days she and Anna Marie had talked of many things, and Betsy, with nothing but intuition to go by, had been interested in how often the mustanger had come into their conversations.

Shortly before sunrise the men had eaten breakfast at the bunkhouse and were ready to ride north and see if the two herds of cattle had found one another, otherwise there was little to do. Life seemed back to normal. Castleton had been the last to leave the bunkhouse and was still saddling up when Betsy appeared in the barn doorway, again wearing her shawl.

He smiled at her as he dropped the stirrup on the left side and gathered his reins.

She replied with an answering smile. "Good morning. Miz Miller would like to see you."

He looped the reins around the saddle pole and they left the barn together. At the main house the fragrance of a woman-cooked breakfast lingered as Betsy went through to the kitchen and Anna Marie faced Castleton from over by the old stone fireplace with the portrait of her husband above it.

"Chet said you had a little trouble," she said.

He smiled. "Good morning to you, too. A little trouble which might have been worse except for Sheriff Alvarado and some possemen arriving."

She seemed unsure of what he might know about her involvement in that and asked another question. "You got all the cattle?"

Instead of immediately replying he walked over and fished out the crumpled bill of sale for her to read.

She studied both sides, not once but twice,

and raised her eyes to his face. "How many had they branded?"

"About twenty head. They were hard at it when we arrived."

"I warned you about Douglas."

"Yes, you sure did, but the way things were going, we wouldn't have needed the sheriff."

She went to a chair and sat down still holding the bill of sale. "That's one of those situations where a person can never be sure, wasn't it?"

He shrugged. "Maybe. Anyway, you have the bill of sale giving you full title to all the misbranded cattle. . . . And with Pete Fincher gone that pretty well ends it."

"Fincher is gone?"

He regarded her wide-eyed look and decided Chet had not mentioned the lynching last night. "Lynched in town sometime after the sheriff had to go hunt horse thieves."

She returned to studying the bill of sale and Ken shifted his weight from one leg to the other leg as he also said, "We had in mind going north to make sure the cattle are back where they should be."

She looked up, finally. "Yes, of course," she said absently. The lynching had hit her hard. There had been other lynchings when her husband had been alive and while she had ambiguous feelings about any kind of hangings not done in accordance with the law, her husband had told her several times that when an outlaw was apprehended it was common and traditional custom to hang them on the spot.

He said, "I'd better be getting along."

She arose from the chair, in command again, "There was something in particular I wanted to talk to you about."

He nodded. He had wondered when Betsy first appeared down at the barn what her summons had meant. But since he'd been fully occupied since leaving the yard he had not thought about this subject.

"I need another rider, Ken. I told you that, and you seemed to agree that beginning with the spring calving, it'd be necessary."

He looked past her to the empty yard and the sun-bright range beyond. "Suppose," he said, "we try it."

"You'll stay?"

"For a while, anyway." As he said this he smiled and dropped his hat atop his head.

She smiled back. "Am I allowed to thank you for all you've done, including this?"

He regarded her for a long time. When she was standing like that, looking directly at him, it was hard to be objective. He finally said, "I'm kind of simple, Miz Miller —"

"Anna Marie. If that's too much, just plain Anna. I've been called Anna most of my life."

He went on as though she had not spoken.

"I like to handle one thing at a time. Anyway, you've fed me an' my horse and all . . ."

She gave up. "I'm very grateful, anyway." She went to the door and held it open until he had passed out to the veranda. As he nodded and started down off the porch in the direction of the barn, she rolled her eyes, muttered something not at all complimentary about men, and turned abruptly when Betsy appeared. Anna Marie remembered an earlier incident when someone in the kitchen, which had no door between it and the parlor, had heard a conversation.

Betsy said, "He is so . . . obstinate."

Anna Marie almost laughed. She put her arm around the girl's shoulders and until Ken was loping northward on his leggy bay horse, neither of them said anything further. When he was very distant Anna Marie gave Betsy a final squeeze and released her to say, "But we aren't without wiles, are we, honey?"

By the time Ken found the vaqueros and Chet Conners it was midafternoon. They were sitting in tree-shade holding the reins of dozing horses. They watched him ride up and swing to the ground before he said, "Had a little delay. Are the critters together?"

Chet answered because neither Gregorio nor Hernan' made any attempt to, they were regarding Castleton from expressionless faces.

"Pretty much," Chet replied, ready to arise.

"You didn't tell the woman about Fincher, Chet."

"No. Betsy would get upset an' I figured someone else could tell Miz Miller. . . . You told her?"

"Yeah."

Hernan' and Gregorio arose beating dust and dead leaves off their britches. They went to snug up the cinches of their horses and just before mounting Hernan' looked at Ken Castleton. "You are going to stay?" he asked.

"For a while, anyway, Hernan'."

"You told her that?"

"Yeah. Why?"

The *mayordomo* swung astride and was evening up his reins as he said, "For no reason, *compañero*."

The conversation on the ride back was mostly about cattle, the range, and the amount of benefit of that storm, and how there was fresh grass sprouting already and it would make cattle washy for at least a month or so.

The employees of THORNDIKE PRESS hope you have enjoyed this Large Print book. All our Large Print books are designed for easy reading — and they're made to last.

Other Thorndike Large Print books are available at your library, through selected bookstores, or directly from us. Suggestions for books you would like to see in Large Print are always welcome.

For more information about current and upcoming titles, please call or mail your name and address to:

THORNDIKE PRESS
PO Box 159
Thorndike, Maine 04986
800/223-6121
207/948-2962